Six Spooky Stories

Halloween Cozy Collection

Sharon E. Buck, Bellamina Court, Kristen Elizabeth, Juliet E. Sidonie, Lily Stirling, Victoria L.K. Williams

Cool Kids Publishing

Contents

This book is dedicated to
Alessandra Torre, Terezia Barna, and Eva Frediani

Words cannot express my gratitude for what you have created through Inkers Mastermind. We met as strangers, became friends, and became part of something so much larger than ourselves. We have become ripples of your dream. Thank you!

Sharon E. Buck

Through Inkers Mastermind, you have created a fabulous and nurturing community of authors. I am in awe of everything the three of you do! Thank you for your friendship and support!

Bellamie Court

Thank you for creating such a wonderful community of writers! This group has pushed me forward in ways that I could never do on my own. I really appreciate the support and guidance you have given to us as a whole and individually. You are amazing!

Kristin E.

This book owes its existence to your unwavering encouragement, boundless enthusiasm, and steadfast support. You have my deepest appreciation for the remarkable network of authors you have created.

Juliet E. Sidorin

Thank you all so much for cultivating a wonderful community for authors! Inkers has brought so much joy to my life.

Lily Stirling

Writing can be a solitary way of life, but through you and Inkers, I have made great friends and a support system as I have never experienced in any other line of work. Thank you for making this possible.

Victoria LK Williams

Introduction

Your Six Spooky Authors met in February of 2024 as members of Alessandra Torre's Inkers Mastermind, an online author group.

We'd barely gotten to know each other's names when the idea sparked for a Halloween-themed cozy collection. After an enthusiastic discussion, we all began planning our individual stories.

Collaborating with fellow Cozy Mystery authors has been spooktacular fun. Each of us brings our own distinct flair to the genre, showcasing remarkable talent.

We're so thankful for a wonderful community of readers. Since reading is such an important part of our lives, this was the perfect opportunity to help future generations unlock new worlds through storytelling. That's why we're donating all our proceeds to Reach Out and Read.

Reach Out and Read focuses on giving age-appropriate books to children in low-income families. They encourage literacy from a young age to help kids unlock the magic of reading.

By purchasing our book, your money helps children receive books that are theirs to keep, read, and love.

Thanks for joining our mission, and happy sleuthing!
Sharon, Bellamina, Kristen, Juliet, Lily, & Victoria

Chapter One

Ghouls Just Wanna Have Fun

Sharon E. Buck

"She's dead! She's dead!" The Wicked Witch of the West, aka Wanda, was screaming, and her stuffed flying monkeys were bouncing around her head as she ran into the middle of the gym floor. I was right in the middle of doing my soon-to-be immortalized Monster Bash dance for YouTube when the shrieking of Wanda interrupted my rhythm.

Thinking it was a practical joke, I ignored the screaming. I was trying hard to concentrate on my moves because my dance skills have been compared to a very frightened baby elephant stomping on a cockroach in the past. Two semi-hop steps to the left, arms up in the kitty-cat pose with my hands dangling from my wrists, then two semi-hops to the right with my arms still up in the kitty-cat pose. I think I finally have those dance moves down.

Maybe it's sad that a thirty-something-year-old female hasn't learned to dance any better than she did in high school. Whatever, I make the effort to dance and it's always fun to catch up with other classmates once a quarter.

Tommy, costumed in Ben Affleck's orange and white DunKings outfit from the Super Bowl Dunkin Donuts commercial, was doing some version of the Franken-step or maybe it was the Werewolf Wiggle or the Zombie Shuffle, I don't know. We weren't dancing in sync together.

He shouted over the music, "Inky Pinky, what's wrong with the Wicked Witch?" Everyone around us was doing some type of body gyrations never learned in a formal dance class. I think everyone thought the Wicked Witch's screaming was a practical joke. Made sense to me that she would scream "She's dead. She's dead!" since she was dressed as a character from the immortal movie The Wizard of Oz. I shrugged, although it may have been mistaken for a dance move.

The more frantic she became, the more those flying monkeys were bouncing around her head and shoulders. I had no clue how she had attached them to her costume. I was a little envious. I went as the Cereal Killer where I had little mini-boxes of cereal with plastic knives stuck in them. I was wearing jeans and a gray tee shirt with white lettering that said, "All Write, All Write, All Write." Somehow that seemed appropriate for a mystery writer. I knew I wasn't going to win the costume parade; plus, I wanted to be comfortable.

As the song ended, Wanda was now borderline hysterically screaming, "She's dead! She's dead!" People began to pay attention to her. Murmurs were heard throughout the crowd.

"Who's dead?"

"How much has the Wicked Witch had to drink?"

"Is she at it again? What's wrong with that girl?"

"See, this is the reason why we shouldn't have alcohol at a reunion."

The DJ stopped the music. "This is DJ Groovy Giggles. May I have everyone's attention? Apparently, there's been a medical emergency with the newly crowned Miss Monster Bash." He cracked up laughing. Next Halloween reunion, we should probably stipulate no alcohol for the DJ. He was in the deep throes of a snort laugh. He was inhaling through his nose sounding almost like a baby pig and had tears running down his face. This, of course, caused all the rest of our group to burst into laughter.

The rest of us were turning to each other, asking questions, and were confused.

Tommy asked, "Isn't Jaimie Miss Monster Bash?" Rolling his eyes, he snorted, "She's as healthy as a horse. She golfs and plays tennis weekly. What does 'DJ Groovy Giggles,'" yes, he air quoted, "know about her?"

DJ Groovy Giggles finally managed to compose himself. "The police and the ambulance will be here shortly. No one may leave."

Pushing whatever buttons on his mixers and turntable boxes to make the songs continue, he did, and the requisite disco ball hanging from the gym's rafter slowly twirled around. People were milling around and still dancing or, at least, twisting their hips and flailing their arms around in some semi-rhythmic variation of rocking out to the music, while questions were buzzing through-out the gym.

After the third song, the police arrived. A few of us were silent at the sight. I guess the Wicked Witch of the West hadn't been kidding. Was Jaimie, Miss Monster Bash, really dead?

After conferring with the organizers for a few moments, one of the officers ran his hand through his short-cropped hair. This was a sign of frustration. How did I know this priceless bit of trivia? Well, I am a mystery writer and a research geek. Somewhere in my Google travels, I had stumbled into a rabbit hole of physical actions that paired up nicely with whatever emotion someone was trying to suppress. It's usually done subconsciously.

One of the cuter officers - there were three of them in our midst now - took the microphone, tapped on it a couple of times, and I'm sure DJ Groovy Giggles did this on purpose, the microphone squealed. Everyone jerked their heads back like an icepick had been plunged deep into their ear.

"We need everyone who was in the costume parade to line up." A collective groan went up from the crowd.

Was the man nuts? We'd had the costume parade at the begin-ning of the Monster Bash, and it lasted a while since probably one hundred costumed adults had walked on the blood-red carpet decorated with little lighted pumpkins every few feet. We were all now hot and sweaty, and some of the costumes weren't quite as pristine as they had been at the beginning of the party.

Some of these folks were beyond competitive about their Hal-loween costume. Let me just say that whatever nasty traits some of these people had in high school, they've had fifteen years to perfect them. Some of these folks I didn't like then and, unlike fine wine, they hadn't improved with age, which meant I wasn't overly fond of them now either. Even though we were all in our early thirties, some of these people had never grown up or they had become old before their retirement years or they had turned into their parents. In short, there weren't that many single, fun friends anymore.

"Tommy..."

"I'm the DunKing, Inky Pinky." He rolled his eyes at me. I had to admit he did have that kind of Ben Affleck vibe. He had grown his beard for a month so it could fill in nicely. I had proposed to color it in with my mascara but apparently that was an inappropriate gender offer. He was highly insulted.

Rumors were starting to float around about what had happened to Jaimie, Miss Monster Bash, if she were really dead. Maybe it was a practical joke after all. Everyone was still snickering and thinking this was a variation of a murder mystery game instead of an actual death in our midst.

I heard someone say, "She got drunk and fell into the punch bowl." I knew that wasn't true because the Good Witch Glinda aka Polly wouldn't have allowed that to happen. Polly was a devout Baptist who loudly proclaimed to anyone who would listen that "alcohol would never touch her lips." She was right, alcohol never touched her lips. She drank it through a straw in the privacy of her own home.

Polly guarded that punch bowl like one of her ill-behaved progenies. Thou shalt not touch or pour anything into that bowl that wasn't sanctified.

Then the rumor was Miss Monster Bash had over-indulged in some cheap illegal street pharmaceuticals. I seriously doubted that. Jaimie was one of the most popular girls from high school and was now a highly esteemed online social media mogul. She was also the proud trophy wife of a very prominent attorney in our small town. The woman always dressed perfectly and was on the board of directors for virtually every social group in town. She wasn't about to do anything that would jeopardize her social standing in our community.

Jaimie had been voted Most Likely to Succeed in high school. She was the quintessential tall, leggy, blonde with a smile that made all of the boys fall in love with her and girls borderline hate her, yet want to be her. She also had the competitive drive that could have made her a shark on the TV show Shark Tank. The woman could breathe the air and turn it into gold. She knew how to make money. She was a MINK – married income no kids.

"Inky Pinky!" My nickname from my sophomore year had never gone away. It was an unfortunate incident with fingerprinting in journalism class where the ink had not completely come off my pinky finger and I apparently touched everything in the classroom but the teacher. My fingerprint was everywhere, and old, crusty Mrs. Banks had looked over the top of her glasses and snapped, "Well, aren't you the inky pinky one." The nickname stuck.

I had to keep reminding myself over the years that Inky Pinky was vastly superior to my other nickname through grade school and junior high. It was M&M. My real name is Mona Madonna. I don't think my parents liked me. Of course, being the last of seven children, maybe they just ran out of names. I'm sure you can understand why a nickname was much preferable to my real name of Mona. I still cringe when I think about the nicknames kids could have come up with on that.

Turning my wayward thoughts back to Tommy, "What do you think happened?"

He shrugged. "Time for us to line up in the costume parade... again."

The cute police officer came over to where our little group of Tommy, Olivia, Danny, and I were standing. His nameplate said "Tinley."

"Officer Tinley, what's going on?" I was smiling. He wasn't.

"Please, just line up and tell me your, ah, character name and your real name."

He wasn't going to be any fun. "I'm the Cereal Killer and my name is Inky Pinky."

He took a deep breath and slowly let it out through his nose. "What's your real name?"

I hadn't used it in so long I had almost forgotten it; plus, it's always fun to mess with a cop. That's what happens in a small rural Southern town where everybody knows everybody else. "It's Mona Bond."

Tinley had been looking at the costume parade names list that the organizer, the Countess of Creepiness, had given him. He glanced up. "Are you James Bond's sister?"

My parents obviously had a perverted sense of humor when it came to naming their offspring. I think they kept producing kids just to give us offbeat names so that we'd have to learn how to fend for ourselves and, thus, making us better people for the harsh realities of life. None of my siblings were amused at their names either.

"Yes, Jim is my older brother." I deliberately didn't say James. "Aren't you Kyle's brother?"

Officer Tinley just grinned. It's a small town. If you couldn't connect someone in two names, you weren't from here.

"Is Jaimie really dead?" I asked him. "A lot of comments are being made that it's part of a murder mystery game."

Tinley shook his head. "Unfortunately, it's not a rumor. This isn't a game."

He continued down his list and marking names off.

A few of us were huddled together talking. Tommy, the DunKing asked, "Wasn't Jaimie a diabetic? Maybe she drank too much punch and that caused some type of reaction."

"That would be Miss Monster Bash to you," I giggled.

Some of our other classmates had joined our group and nodded. Todd, a former defensive end for the University of Florida's National Football Championship team, was dressed as an Ohio tourist wearing a Florida shirt with flamingos and palm trees on a pale green background, baggie beige shorts hanging to his knees, white tube socks pulled halfway up his hairy legs, and sandals. "I think she had to take insulin shots a couple of times a day," he said.

"How come her husband, Steve, wasn't here with her?" asked Berta, dressed as a waitress from Metro Diner. I suspected she had come to the party after her shift was over. She had a tray full of drinks which she admonished us to wait our turn so she wouldn't lose control of the tray.

DJ Groovy Giggles had started the music again. This time it was very low. While it was probably inappropriate to start dancing again, we all did so.

The microphone squealed again. Officer Tinley tapped it a couple of times. "Attention, attention. We're going to take statements from each one of you. No one can leave."

Dianna, dressed as a pineapple with a tiara that read 'Queen of Fruits,' immediately howled a protest. "I have a babysitter. Who's gonna pay for the extra time?"

Noticing several other moms nodding in agreement, I waved my hand. "Officer Tinley, Officer Tinley, how long is all of this going to take?"

He glanced over at me and then promptly walked to the far corner of the gym to question Dianna, Queen of Fruits, first. The other officers had gone to their respective corners with different classmates to question them.

Our once beautifully decorated gym with large black plastic cauldrons with green mist periodically rising from them, the tarantula black balloon sculpture tall enough for us to stand under and take pictures, the cheesy silly string sprayed over the Happy

Halloween and Monster Bash banners, carved pumpkins galore, plastic tombstones stuck to the wood floor with duct tape – Good Witch Glinda aka Polly the Baptist thought it would be a good idea to put the names of several of our classmates who were no longer with us in the natural sense on the tombstones. Why? No one knew. Maybe it was her way of remembering them. I was going to have a field day including all of this in my next novel. I already had a title in mind, The Grim Reaper's Guide to Getting Away with Murder.

"You're plotting and planning again, aren't you?" laughed my BFF Terri who was dressed as Holy Guacamole and now standing at my elbow.

I eyed her costume. "You're an avocado with a halo and wings? Green is not your color, Terri. Why didn't you go with our original idea of being a Crazy Cat Lady with the bathrobe and stuffed cats pinned to it? Also, where have you been? I haven't seen you since I got here."

"Inky Pinky, it was too hot, and I couldn't move around in it very easily. I've been here. You've just been busy with Tommy and..."

"DunKing." Tommy was going to stick to that all night long.

Terri seemed to be a little nervous, maybe even a little defensive when I asked where she had been all night. Normally, she and Jaimie were the queens of any social event. They liked being in the spotlight. They competed for the title to anything and everything in town. They had been going after the same titles since we were in junior high school.

I hadn't seen Terri on the dance floor all night. She was a good dancer, and everyone liked to dance with her. "Terri, why…?

She leaned over and whispered in my ear. "I didn't feel well enough to dance. I think I may be pregnant again."

"Really?" I jerked my head back with a big smile on my face. "When were you going to tell me?"

She let her eyes rove over the dance floor. "I haven't told you anything because, well, Josh and I are having problems and I'm, I'm not, I'm just not sure about this one."

I inwardly groaned. Terri was always dramatic. This was probably the fifth or sixth time she'd told me she thought she was pregnant this year alone. I didn't believe her. She just wanted sympathy for whatever was going on in her life. She also waited until the most inappropriate or stressful times to tell me things like this. I always offered her my support, which I did this time also.

"Don't you even think about it! I'll help you. This is what best friends are for. We'll make this work." I paused, grabbed hold of her hands, and leaned back toward her to whisper, "Is Josh fooling around again? Who is it this time?"

Tears sprang up, "I'm not sure. He's always bragged to me in the past about who it was, but he hasn't done it this time. What am I going to do, Inky Pinky?"

I hugged her and asked the same question I always do. "Why do you stay with Josh when he's always running around on you? I've never been able to figure that out."

She was quietly sobbing now but no one was paying any attention. "I'm an economic slave, you know that. I don't have any job skills, I have to stay home with my babies, and…" the tears were streaming down her face, "I love Josh. He treats us well and he's a good provider for the family. It's just his running around that I hate."

Aarrgghh! I just wanted to slap her silly. She was too good to put up with this from Josh. I'd known about his running around on her for several years but, cough, cough, Terri wasn't exactly Miss Faithful either. They deserved each other - I guess.

Officer Tinley suddenly showed up at my elbow. "You," he pointed at the far corner of the gym, "go over there and let Officer Durbin get your statement."

"Sir," I was trying to be respectful, "since you're questioning us, I think we all should ask our attorneys first before we answer any questions."

Poker face set in granite is what popped into my mind with Officer Tinley. "If you don't have anything to hide, why would you mind giving a statement to the police, Miss Mona Bond?" This was almost a sneer from him. "Also, Miss Bond, you've had ample time to call your attorney since we've been here. What's your point?"

Actually, I had already texted my attorney. Apparently, she had nothing else to do on a Saturday night in a small, sleepy, Southern town but to answer clients' text messages. She had told me it was okay to talk to the police since I didn't know anything.

I held my hands up. "Just asking, that's all. I'm happy to cooperate." I smiled. Okay, it was a cheesy smile, but I was trying to be reasonably polite; annoying, yes. Why? Because I could be. I have a streak of rebelliousness against authority in general. I blame it on my parents naming me Mona Madonna Bond. Hey, it's as good a reason as any. I don't know why I'm like this, but I also don't feel the need to go to therapy over it either.

He just pointed to the corner where Officer Durbin was looking around the gym, probably bored out of his mind. I strolled across the floor.

"What can I answer for you, Officer?"

He asked a few questions about where I was, what I had been doing, and if I had drunk any of the punch. He didn't ask about the snacks, and that was interesting. To my mind, that meant only one thing. Jaimie had died by drinking the punch.

Yes, I had drunk the punch. It was your standard Baptist non-alcoholic juice that is liberally served at Vacation Bible Schools throughout the United States – red Hawaiian Punch mixed with ginger ale. Yes, we had all brought mini-bottles of our favorite adult liquid libation and mixed it in the red go-cups. No different now as adults than what we had done in high school. Some things never change.

"How well did you know Jaimie?" asked the officer jotting down some notes.

"Jaimie, Miss Monster Bash? I've known her since junior high school. We grew up together."

"Do you know anyone who might have wanted to do her harm? Didn't like her, may have even hated her?" His pen was poised to write down anything of importance that I might say.

"No. I think everybody liked her." I'm sure she probably did have someone who didn't like her, but I didn't know of any.

I was dismissed and made my way back to the group. Cyndi Lauper's "Girls Just Wanna Have Fun" was playing, Tommy and I started dancing again. I looked around for Terri. She was standing in the back corner talking to Tinley and another officer. She saw me and made gigantic wave motions with her hands for me to come over. Officer Tinley turned to see who she was waving at. I pointed at myself. What was going on that Terri needed my help?

Tinley nodded for me to come over. I handed my red go-cup to Tommy. He was my one male friend who I knew wouldn't spit in it while I wasn't looking. Also, it probably wasn't a wise idea to take a freshly refilled cup of Baptist punch and rum over to the officers. None of us had over-indulged, well, DJ Groovy Giggles had but he doesn't count since he wasn't a classmate, but still...I didn't want to give the cops any reason not to let me drive home in my own vehicle.

"So," Tinley cleared his throat, "how long have you known Terri Derschell?"

Holy Guacamole! Okay, that was a bad pun on her costume, but this wasn't good. Terri never used her maiden name. Why didn't she tell Tinley her married name was Hargrove? Her eyes were a little wider than normal and rivers of sweat – it was past the perspiration phase of bodily fluids – were running down the sides of her face.

"Inky Pinky, I told them I wasn't feeling well."

I nodded, looking at Officer Tinley and the other policeman. I couldn't see his badge name. "She told me she wasn't feeling well--"

Terri interrupted me, "Earlier in the evening." She nervously laughed, "It's that time of the month, guys."

I guess she figured that would make the police leave her alone. Me, on the other hand, wondered what was up with the misinformation. Although we had been friends forever and three days, I couldn't read her mind to know what she wanted me to do.

Good Witch Glinda popped up next to me and announced, "Officers, I happened to remember that Wanda, she's dressed as the Wicked Witch of the West, has hated Jaimie for years. You might want to check her alibi out."

Really, Miss Goody Two Shoes? You're going to throw Wanda under the bus? I'm betting Wanda had threatened to spike the punch, she wouldn't have, and Good Witch Glinda still felt the need to get back at her. There were people's lives at stake here, not some petty annoyance at each other.

Tinley semi-grimaced, then glanced at his notes. "I've already talked to her, and she said you two had gotten into an argument about how much ginger ale was to be in the punch. She did admit she had taunted you with 'you're full of fudge nuggets' and stomped off. Is that true, Good Witch Glinda or should I call you Polly now?"

I couldn't help it, I started to chuckle. That was so Wanda, to get mad at someone and, instead of actual curse words, use terms like 'fudge nuggets,' 'shish kebob,' or 'mother of pearl' to indicate her displeasure. She was highly excitable but harmless. She wouldn't hurt anyone.

Polly glared at the officer. Her jaw clenched. "Yes."

"So, maybe you're just mad at her, huh?" Tinley looked like he wanted to be anywhere but here. "And, maybe, Wanda didn't really hate Jaimie. Is that a possibility?"

The Good Witch Glinda façade disappeared from Polly's face before she answered, "I'm going back to the snack bar area if you need me." She stomped off.

Tinley wiped his forehead with his hand. He turned back to Terri. "Aren't you married to Josh Hargrove?"

It's a small town. We all pretty much knew who was married to whom, how many times someone's been married, who's fooling around, and fifty other million vital pieces of worthless information to spread lies and gossip about.

Terri's shoulders dropped, a tear slid down her face, she looked at the ground, and nodded.

Tinley must have a heart because he gently said, "It'll be okay."

She sort of bobbed her head.

"You two can go." He turned, "Oh, wait. Who is the guy dressed up as Bob Ross, the TV artist painter guy?"

Terri and I looked at each other and burst out laughing. "His name is really Bob Ross."

Grinning, I added, "Bob's really an engineer and, yes, that's really his own curly hair."

Once we had gotten far enough away from the officers, I asked, "Terri, what's up? Why are you lying? That's a really dangerous thing to do."

"Am I a good actress or what?" She giggled. "I didn't think it was any of his business. I'm fine."

Catching the surprised look on my face, "Stop that! What I told you was true. I might be pregnant."

"Have you done the pee-on-the-stick test yet?"

"Tomorrow, I'll do it tomorrow," she promised.

Tommy had consumed my go-cup contents while I was talking with the officers. "I think I know what happened to Jaimie."

Doing a side-eye glance, "Yeah, Mr. DunKing. What happened?"

"Well, me and Danny here..." Danny, Tommy's BFF, dressed as the Village Idiot complete with a dunce hat with red tassels, white shirt, black and silver vertically striped pants, purple and white horizontal striped socks up to his knees with black pointy-toed shoes, was grinning like the proverbial Cheshire Cat, "think that the Cupcake Queen of Sweets did it. She probably told Jaimie that her cupcakes didn't have any sugar in them which, of course, was a lie. Jaimie ate too much sugar, went into a diabetic coma, and died."

"You, Mr. DunKing, and the Village Idiot here..."

"Hey, hey!" protested Danny, "I'm not an idiot."

Olivia, his latest sweetie, in her French Maid's outfit, murmured, "I told him not to wear that costume."

I laughed and looked around at everyone who was still here. "You mean to tell me that absolutely no one else noticed the Cupcake Queen of Sweets gave Jaimie a cupcake or two or three based on your outstanding observational skills? Oh, pul-leaze, guys, give me a break."

Posing in her cute little French Maid's outfit, Olivia took her feather duster and waved it around, poking Tommy, Danny, and me with it. "It's probably something so simple that killed her that everyone is overlooking it. Who was she hanging out with? That's who the cops need to be looking at."

Tommy shrugged, "We've all been hanging out with each other all night. I mean Jaimie only died after she was voted as Miss Monster Bash. That Miss Liberty costume was off the charts. I heard she had ordered it online several months ago."

Since our sort of class reunions happened once a quarter and we knew the "Ghouls Just Wanna Have Fun" theme for the Halloween party, we had all been planning what to wear for months. All of the other get-togethers didn't involve costumes. They were the typical small-town casual wear – tee shirts, nice shirts, and jeans.

Olivia, who had been behind us a year in school, asked, "Who came up with the 'Ghouls Just Wanna Have Fun' theme?"

I wasn't sure. I looked at Tommy who shrugged. "I don't know. Maybe it was Wanda."

"Maybe it was Wanda what?" The Wicked Witch of the West magically appeared next to Danny. He jumped. "What did I do this time?"

Wanda's makeup was a soggy green mess. She had been crying. I couldn't blame her. After all, she had found Jaimie dead in the ladies' restroom.

Smiling, I asked, "Were you the one who came up with the theme for this Monster Bash party?"

"I don't remember who came up with the name," she brightened up for a moment, although the tear-streaked green makeup now kind of looked like green boogers on her face. "It's a great name though, right?"

We all grinned and gave our thumbs-up approval. Wanda didn't hang out with our gang very often and I thought she might go hang out with another group. I was wrong. It was obvious Wanda wasn't going anywhere.

"Wanda, what happened? Are you okay?" I gently asked her. I did pat her on the shoulder although those darn monkeys were bobbing around like mosquitoes at an all-you-can-eat-smorgasbord of naked arms in the Florida summertime. I didn't want a monkey to get me.

"The cops told me I couldn't say anything." Her eyes welled up with tears again. She made a move to hug me. No, no, no! I didn't want those monkeys touching me! They were weird-looking and had little googly eyes. Wanda may have made them at one of her arts and crafts classes.

Olivia, bless her heart, jumped over and gave Wanda the needed hug. Two monkeys got stuck in her French Maid's lace apron. We all helped to untangle the monkeys after the hug; well, except for me. I'm not touching those things! Remember, the monkeys lifted Dorothy up and flew away with her in the Wizard of Oz. I didn't want to take the chance they might really come to life and drag me off to God knows where.

"Now, honey, it's okay for you to tell us. We're your friends and," Olivia paused, looking to see where the cops were, "no one's here to silence you."

Oh, good move, Olivia. I might need to get to know her better.

Wanda sniffled a couple of times and then looked at each of us. "Jaimie had been over at the snack table. She was talking with everyone and laughing. You know how she always made everyone feel special, right? Anyway, she had a go-cup in her hand, took a drink, set it down, and went to the ladies' restroom. Me and Good Witch Glinda were trash-talking about how much ginger ale needed to be in that nasty Hawaiian Punch. Why is she always in charge of that mess?"

We laughed; we felt the same way. Tommy offered, "I think she just brings the Hawaiian Punch and ginger ale with her everywhere she goes. She mixes everything together when she arrives at whatever event she's attending, and no one has the cajónes to tell her no more Baptist punch."

Danny, Olivia, and I agreed, "Probably so."

"Anyway, the newspaper photographer was here and wanted to take Jaimie's picture."

You had to give Wanda props because she always managed to make sure our reunions made the local newspaper – all eight pages of it.

"I looked around, didn't see her, and Polly said she hadn't seen her either. The last time I saw her was when she went to the restroom, and I remember thinking she couldn't possibly still be in there because a good twenty or thirty minutes had passed."

Wanda broke down crying again. Her makeup was a disaster, and I really couldn't look at her face because I was afraid I'd burst out laughing. At least Terri wasn't here to egg me on.

"Anyway, I went into the bathroom and there she was. She was splayed out like the Statue of Liberty only on the floor and she still had her Miss Monster Bash trophy in her right hand." Wanda sniffled some more. "Her Miss Liberty torch was lying next to her."

I had to turn away because I had laugh tears zooming down my cheeks at the speed of light at the thought of the Miss Monster Bash trophy being compared to the Miss Liberty torch and the Statue of Liberty. My shoulders were shaking with laughter. Wanda mistakenly took my actions as one of extreme distress caused by the death of a former classmate. She hugged me. Those darn, fudge nuggets, shish kabobbed monkeys touched the back of my head and I totally became unglued. I jumped, I hollered, and an adult curse word or two may or may not have unintentionally escaped my lips.

Danny did give all appearances of the Village Idiot by falling on the floor laughing. Olivia wasn't much better and was no help this time. Tommy did the Ben Affleck DunKing prancing knee hop. Me? I fell on the floor in the fetal position totally forgetting I had tiny little cereal boxes with plastic knives in them pinned all over my clothes. The little plastic knives were stabbing me in various parts of my body and causing a great deal of pain. Rolling over only caused more discomfort with those knives. Whoever said plastic breaks easily never has done this.

And, Wanda, trying to be helpful, loomed over me with those monkeys flopping around like they had mated with the Energizer Bunny.

I was screaming and trying to cover my head. I finally opened my tightly, squeezed shut eyes as I felt myself being hoisted to my feet. Officer Tinley was staring into my face like he might need to Baker Act me. I wasn't that crazy!

Stifling a grin, he asked, "Are you okay?"

I had gone over the edge of sanity and was blathering about the monkeys and how they touched me when he handed me a go-cup of that nasty Baptist punch. I choked and spit it out. In the middle of his dark blue shirt. I didn't mean to, it just happened.

"Someone needs to take," he coughed after looking down at his soiled shirt, "Inky Pinky home."

Leaning toward me, Tinley grinned, "How much rum have you had?"

I was still sputtering, "Obviously, not enough but I'm okay to drive."

He rolled his eyes. "All of you go home. We'll be in touch."

Danny and Olivia offered to take Wanda home. To say she was distraught was an understatement. Between finding Jaimie dead and me having a total emotional breakdown because of her monkeys flying around her head, her self-confidence and self-esteem were probably at an all-time low. She didn't have an abundance of either one of those qualities to begin with.

Two days later, I got a phone call from Terri. I was happy to hear from her.

"Yo, girl, what's up? I haven't heard from you since the party. Are you pregnant? Tell me what's going on."

"Bestie, I'm not PG."

Honestly, I was relieved for her. If she and Josh were having problems in their marriage, the last thing they needed was another baby. Although I strongly suspected this was just another one of her fake pregnancy announcements because she wanted sympathy from me about her marriage.

"So, what's up?"

"Not much."

Okay, this wasn't like Terri. She was very bubbly and outgoing, not quiet and demur. I wasn't sure how to proceed with our conversation. It felt one-sided to me.

"Terri, how come you weren't in the costume parade at the Monster Bash? Your Holy Guacamole outfit was great. I think you might have even beaten Jaimie this time."

She snapped, "I told you. I wasn't feeling well. Besides, I always come in second. What was the point?"

We changed topics and chatted about nothing for another couple of minutes. Then I asked, "Are you going to Jaimie's funeral tomorrow?"

"Well, not in a Holy Guacamole costume!"

We laughed.

The funeral was a very nice affair. Jaimie's husband, Steve, had it catered at the Women's Club. Just like every other social function in town, Polly was there with her Baptist punch.

We - Tommy, Danny, Olivia, Wanda, and I - met up for coffee after the funeral. Terri didn't show up for Jaimie's funeral but that really wasn't unusual. She didn't attend most funerals. As she so eloquently put it, "The only funeral I have to attend is my own."

We were still giggling about Polly and her punch when Officer Tinley walked into the coffee shop just as we sat down. I waved at him; he ignored me. I was just trying to be nice. I guess he was still upset that I had accidentally spit on his uniform shirt. I poked Tommy. He rolled his eyes, groaned, and walked over to Tinley. He looked around Tommy and stared at our group for a moment before getting his coffee and walking back over with Tommy.

He acknowledged our presence with an uplifting of his chin. Was that urban for 'yo, what's up'?

Sitting down across from me, he asked, "Have you seen or talked to Terri lately...or do you want to talk to your attorney first?"

We all grinned. I had filled them in with my quasi-tongue-in-cheek comment about attorneys at the Monster Bash party.

"Actually, I talked with her yesterday. We just chitchatted for a few minutes and that was it."

"Did she say anything about why she wasn't in the costume parade?"

I shrugged. "Just that she wasn't feeling well and didn't want to do it."

We talked about a few new things happening around town and that was it. He left to go back on duty.

"You know, I kind of wondered the same thing about Terri," said Danny slowly. "She and Jaimie competed for everything. It did seem odd that she wasn't in the parade."

Wanda took a sip of her hot chocolate. "That's probably because she was late coming in. She didn't arrive until the parade was almost over."

The radar that was circling on my head had gone from a happy-go-lucky merry-go-round speed to something that was threatening to spin off my head and go to the moon and back. Everyone looked at Wanda.

"What do you mean she came in late? Terri's always on time. In fact, she's almost always early." I was confused. I hadn't seen Terri at the beginning of the party. Mainly because I was so focused on having a good time dancing with Tommy. I like to dance, just because I have no rhythm means absolutely nothing.

Polly came through the coffee shop's entrance door like a Category 4 hurricane. She had a wild-eyed look when she saw us. "Are y'all having a meeting and didn't include me?" she demanded. Turning to Wanda, she snapped, "Haven't you been arrested yet?"

Wanda's mouth hung open and she started to cry. "What am I being arrested for?"

"Murder, you stupid wench."

Usually, I avoid confrontation at all costs, but today I'd had it. I stood up, I was taller than Polly. Maybe I could squash her like a bug.

"Inky Pinky, you stay out of this." Polly pointed her finger at me, poked me three times, and turned facing Wanda. "Wanda's a liar and a murderer. I told the cops how you had been in and out of the bathroom umpteen times. How you had a bathrobe with you. I know you were jealous of her."

"Polly, you know if you pop me with that finger of yours one more time, it's technically assault, don't you?" My temper flared up. "Also, I'm telling everyone a secret about you and your husband." I was mad.

That probably wasn't the right thing to do or say when there was an irate female standing in front of me, but it did distract her from bashing Wanda. I wasn't so sure if Polly was going to send me to heaven on the Monster Bash Express. Tommy was trying to pull me down into my chair.

"What's your so-called secret?" she hissed. "We have nothing to hide."

I smirked. "What about your hubby going to the far end of the county to buy...sherry that's not used for cooking."

Everyone gasped and then laughed. I thought Polly was going to explode. "You'd better have proof of that, Inky Pinky, or I'll sue you for slander."

I held up my cell phone. "I have a picture of Dickie in The Old Tyme Liquor Store and he's standing at the counter swiping his card with two, count them, two bottles of sherry."

She went to grab for my phone, but I had plopped back down in my seat because of Tommy's pulling on me. She missed my phone, but face planted on the tabletop. I suppose I should say I was sorry that happened, but I wasn't, and I laughed instead.

Wanda was still crying, and Olivia was trying to comfort her. Hiccupping, Wanda managed to get out, "I didn't kill Jaimie. I wasn't jealous of her. She was always so nice to me."

I guess the coffee shop people had called the cops because Officer Tinley was back again. He wasn't amused.

"What's going on here?"

I gave him the short version. Polly was gingerly touching her nose, threatening all sorts of things against all of us. Tinley led her to a table several tables over. She sat there for a moment, shaking her head, and then got up to go to her car. She slowly maneuvered around the drive-thru line and left.

Tinley came back over to us. "Polly's having a bad day. I think Jaimie's death has affected her much more than she's let on."

Okay, I had a little empathy for her. Not a great deal but enough to cut her a break.

"Officer Tinley, she said Wanda was going to be arrested for the murder of Jaimie." I looked quizzically at him, hoping for some type of response one way or the other. I was disappointed.

"That's not up to me, it's up to the powers that be."

Danny chuckled. "A rhyming cop. Are we going to see you on America's Got Talent at any point? Can you rap?"

I'm sure Tinley didn't think much of our sense of humor, but he probably didn't see wonderful people like us on an everyday basis either.

"Inky Pinky, you're the murder expert. What do you think happened?" asked Wanda, her eyes big and wide, after Tinley left.

"Whoa, whoa, whoa! I'm not an expert. I write murder mystery books. They're fiction." I tried to explain. Did I have an idea of what happened? Yes. Was I right? Maybe, possibly, probably not. I didn't want to be right.

Steve, Jaimie's husband, came into the coffee shop. Gone was the normal bounce in his step that we all knew, his body language looked dejected. He saw us, got his coffee, and came over to join us. We all told him how sorry we were about Jaimie. He nodded, silent, looking down in his coffee mug.

He took a deep breath and sighed. "Jaimie was the love of my life. I would give anything to have her still be here."

Steve looked up. "I don't think I was the love of her life though. Do any of y'all know anything about that?"

Shock was an understatement. If the earth had suddenly dropped out from underneath me or anyone else at the table, we couldn't have been more surprised. This is a small town and surely one of us would have heard something if Jaimie had been fooling around on Steve. The only way we wouldn't have heard something would have been because the relationship was so new or that she and her fellow were going out of town for their fun and games.

"Steve," Tommy cleared his throat. "Why weren't you at the Monster Bash?"

Why do guys always clear their throats when they're about to ask an important question? I think it's in their male DNA at birth.

Steve shrugged. "We'd had a fight about a new investment she was doing with some guy. She wire-transferred him a hundred thousand dollars. I hadn't seen the contract, I don't even know what the product or service was, and she wouldn't give me any more details."

"Wait, Steve. You can always look at your checking account and figure out who the money went to." I was sure of this.

"We had our own separate personal and business accounts. That's going to take a bit of time to get things done with the bank."

I shook my head; something wasn't making any sense. "Steve, was the guy local?"

He nodded.

An ugly thought was creeping into my brain. It was only a theory, but it was one I really didn't want the answer to. I wondered if the cops had the same idea I had. If not, maybe I should be a cop and not a mystery writer. After all, it's their job to figure out these things.

I was sure Wanda was the unsuspecting and unknowing key to everything. After a few more minutes of idle chatter, we all left.

Calling Officer Tinley, I left a message with my idea of what had happened to Jaimie. He didn't call back.

I sat up all night writing down everything I could remember. I wanted to talk to Wanda but didn't dare call before eight in the morning because that would just be rude since she wasn't a close friend.

My BFF Terri texted me at seven thirty-two. "Hey, I am so happy! Josh got tickets for our whole family to go to Bolivia. You know, like Butch Cassidy and the Sundance Kid. Anyway, we're on our way to the airport. Catch you later."

I was happy for her. A tear slid down my cheek. I called Wanda at eight on the dot. "Hey, are you free for coffee or breakfast in the next thirty minutes? My treat."

Wanda was enthusiastic and we met at the diner. "Wanda, I have a couple of questions about the Monster Bash."

She beamed, "It was a lot of fun, wasn't it? Well, at least in the beginning when everyone dressed up in their costumes."

Taking a deep breath, I plunged forward with my question. "You got there early, right?"

"Yes."

"When did Terri show up? You had said she was late to the costume parade. I just wondered what time you think she showed up."

Cutting her sausage patty into tiny little squares, she answered, "Oh, Terri was there at the beginning."

Be still, my beating heart. "You said you found a bathrobe in the ladies' restroom, right?"

"Yes, it looked like it had been part of someone's costume, but I guess they changed their mind about wearing it."

"Wanda, when Terri showed up, what was she wearing?" My heart felt like it was in my throat.

"She had on jeans and a tee shirt. She was carrying a garment bag and went into the restroom to change."

I shut my eyes slowly. No, please don't let it be true, I thought. I whispered, "What was her first costume? Was it a bathrobe with little stuffed cats pinned to it and she was going to be the Crazy Cat Lady?"

Wanda looked up, surprised. "Yes, how did you know?"

"No one asked you about the bathrobe or the stuffed cats pinned to it? That maybe it was part of a costume or something?"

"No."

I blinked again slowly. "Were Jaimie and Terri in the restroom together at any time?"

Wanda shrugged. "I don't know. I was kind of surprised when she came out of the bathroom about halfway through the costume parade. She was wearing her Holy Guacamole outfit then."

Trying hard not to scream 'you're a special kind of stupid' at Wanda, I managed to eke out, "Didn't it strike you as odd that Terri had two different outfits for the Monster Bash?"

"No. Several of the other girls had two outfits and they were trying to figure out which one stood the greatest chance of winning."

Okay, that made sense...maybe, sort of.

"Terri was upset though. She thought her Crazy Cat Lady costume was good and some of the other girls were teasing her that it was too plain and wouldn't stand a chance against Jaimie's Statue of Liberty costume. One of the girls told Terri, 'Why bother? You know she's going to be Miss Monster Bash. She wins at everything.' We all kind of giggled."

I shut my eyes and held them shut for a long thirty seconds. Yes, I counted because I was trying not to choke Wanda for not telling the cops everything, or maybe she had.

Opening my eyes, I asked, "You told all of this to the cops, right?"

She smiled. "Yes."

Okay, I might have to take back the stupid part, but I hadn't said it out loud. So that meant it didn't count, right?

I heard the sirens go by as we were sitting there. I was still processing everything in my head and heard Wanda say something, but I wasn't paying attention.

"Do what, Wanda? I'm sorry, I was thinking." I was trying to smile and failing miserably at it.

"Inky Pinky, I said I also told the cops that Terri had given Jaimie a red go-cup right before the parade started."

I shut my eyes, and I could feel the tears making their way south on my face. My phone pinged. Wiping the tears from my eyes, note to self, don't use the same napkin for tears that you've just wiped your lips with that had Tabasco sauce on them. Tommy had texted me. "Josh is dead. Terri and the kids are gone."

I got up from my seat. "Wanda, I've got to make a phone call. I'll be right back."

Walking outside, I called Terri. I had a one-word question for her. "Why?"

She sounded relaxed, cheerful almost. "Why? I was tired of always being number two. Number one, you win. Number three, you're just happy you're in the top three. Number two, you always wonder what it takes to be number one and no matter what you do, you're still number two."

Then an ugliness I had never heard before crept into her voice. "Josh was sleeping with Jaimie. She had given him a hundred thousand dollars for some online money-making scheme he'd come up with. It was one thing for him to sleep around, it was another thing for him to sleep with my number one nemesis. I couldn't take it anymore, Bestie. They both had to go."

She laughed, "It was so easy. I took my electrolyte drink in with me. It had lead acetate in it and I simply poured some in Jaimie's drink. You can't taste it and it acts fairly quickly…" she paused, "or maybe it was another one of those chemicals I looked up online. I took my drink home with me and, as far as I know, the cops still haven't figured it out or, if they have, they have no clue how Jaimie got it."

How could we have been BFFs and I never knew this side of her? She had gone completely over the edge of reality into the land of cray-cray. I was heartbroken. "Girl…Terri…"

"I love you, Bestie. I wish you much success in your writing. Heck," she laughed, "write a bestseller about the Monster Bash party." Pausing for a moment, she whispered, "Bolivia doesn't have an extradition agreement with the U.S., and that hundred thousand dollars will last a really long time there."

Then, in a much louder voice, "I have to go, the plane is boarding. I won't have a phone anymore."

My phone pinged again. Looking at the text message, I couldn't help it, I had to laugh. My BFF still had a sense of humor. There was a little red heart and the words 'ghouls just wanna have fun.'

How could I laugh as the tears were cascading down my cheeks? I felt like I couldn't breathe. The green-eyed monster of jealousy caused Terri to murder two people. I guess Holy Guacamole green is her color after all.

Sharon E. Buck

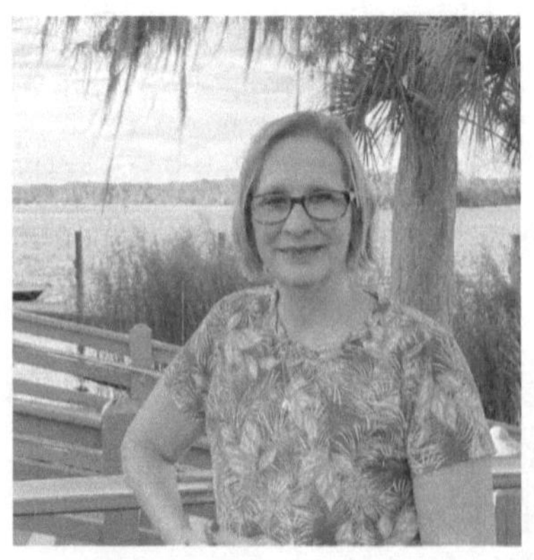

Sharon E. Buck currently resides in Jacksonville, FL where her friends think she sits around eating chocolate bonbons, lying by the pool, and soaking up sunshine. In reality, she sits behind a computer writing words and working hard on a tan from the glowing blue light of her laptop. Her favorite sayings really capture her style – fun, witty, and engaging - "my imagination becomes your entertainment" and "a little sass, a little snark, and a whole lot of silliness." Visit SharonEBuck.com and receive a **FREE** book.

Chapter Two

Murder at the Manor

Bellamina Court

As I waited for Tina and Nikki at the airport, I opened the TNT Girls' email thread.

I am so excited that we are finally getting our girls' weekend! ~Trish

I don't think we have all been together since my bachelorette weekend! I can't wait to see you both! xx, Tina

Remember when we promised we would get together every year?

Ha-ha. Tina got married five years ago. -Nikki

Ah, the naivety of youth, before we realized how little things like

work and family would get in the way. ~Trish

This is the year! It's going to be so much fun! xx, Tina

We were randomly assigned as roommates during our freshman year of college. We quickly became inseparable, always attending parties together, and because our names are Trish, Nikki, and Tina, people started collectively calling us TNT. I swear we had nothing to do with the bomb scare at the Omegas or the fire at Delta. We were explosive, just not literally.

After college, I took a job as an editorial assistant at Palm Pointe Publishing. Last year, they moved me to the Juniper Beach office to work directly with Sylvie Prescott. Nikki ignored her newly earned journalism degree and became a bounty hunter, while Tina opened a boutique shop, married her college sweetheart, Jack, and had twins, all in less than two years. It has been so long since we have all been able to get together. In January, we made it our resolution to find time this year for a girls' weekend.

We found the perfect activity for our time together: a murder mystery experience at the old Beaubien Manor bed-and-breakfast. Okay, so the murder mystery part is just Saturday dinner, but we're meeting tonight to catch up over margaritas. There's so much catching up to be done! I haven't even told them I was fired.

The idea for our weekend adventure actually came from a former college classmate. Being new to the area, I was surprised to run into Lucas at the supermarket. I had no idea he lived in Juniper Beach.

Lucas is the son of the proprietors of Beaubien Manor. His parents retired earlier this year. Lucas and his siblings had their own lives, but he didn't want to give up his parents' dream. The manor has been empty most of the year as Lucas made arrangements to move back to Juniper Beach.

Beaubien Manor isn't quite ready for the grand reopening, but Lucas and his siblings didn't want to miss a year of their annual

Murder Mystery dinner, so they are hosting a soft opening on Halloween.

Relatively new to town, I hadn't heard of the manor, its rich history, or the annual festivities. You know how it is. Once you hear about something, you hear stories about it everywhere. There are several variations of the story, but the basics are the same. In the late 1600s, a pirate captain allegedly buried his treasure somewhere on the property. In 1684, William Beaubien built a home on the land where the treasure was supposedly buried.

Rumor was that every year on Halloween, Captain Sterling's ghost was found digging holes on the property, looking for his lost fortune. The legend continues that once every fifty years, Captain Sterling becomes convinced his treasure was stolen from him and he kills the first person found digging on the property. Over three hundred years later, the holes continue to appear annually on Halloween. Some believe it to be mostly harmless pranks by mischievous teens. Others are adamant that the ghost of Captain Sterling is looking for his buried treasure.

It was easy to spot my best friends at the airport. Nikki's slow saunter countered Tina's quick zigzag around the other passengers as she hurried toward me.

Tina pulled us both into a fierce hug. "Ohmygosh! Itissogoodtoseeyougals!" Her words poured out like a rushing river, practically cascading over each other, nearly impossible to decipher.

"Dang, Tina! I forgot how fast you talk when you're excited," I laughed.

"Yeah, yeah, it's great to see y'all. Now, let's get a drink."

I lightly punched Nikki. "Sometimes, I swear that is the only thing you think about."

"Not true. The whole plane ride here I was thinking about all the fun I could have had with my latest bounty–had I decided to take a detour before turning him in." Nikki wiggled her eyebrows.

"Oh, you are so bad. Tell us more! Married with kids doesn't allow for such, um, imaginations."

I gasped, "Tina, that can't be the case. You and Jack were always sneaking off somewhere."

"Were, past tense. We have two young kids now. Jack works crazy hours, and the boutique takes everything I have left. Enough about me, Trish, how are you?" Tina nudged me with her elbow.

"So, um, about those drinks, the Cantina serves fabulous margaritas."

"Ohh," said Nikki and Tina at the same time.

"The Manor is a couple of miles outside of town. Let's check in, then take an Uber for drinks and dinner."

Tina shoved her finger in my face. "Fine, but don't think you're getting off that easy."

I put up my hands defensively, "Okay, okay."

We hefted our luggage from the Uber and pulled them behind us as we walked up the path to Beaubien Manor. There was a man crouched by the flower beds. He seemed to be setting up Halloween decorations.

"Hello!" we said in unison.

He gave a wave without looking up and continued working.

We walked up the sidewalk that was lined with floating ghost lights. The front lawn was set up like a graveyard, complete with plastic tombstones that had artificial spider webs draped across them. We pushed aside the decorations covering the entrance of the bed-and-breakfast. The waxy fake webs clinging to our arms and the cheap plastic spiders tickling our fingers and catching in our sweaters. We walked to the desk and found a note.

Welcome to Beaubien Manor.

Please enjoy this complimentary bottle of wine.

I'm sorry we couldn't be there to greet you ourselves. Todd and I are getting my house ready for our sister's visit. We have set you up in three rooms on the second floor. You will find your keys in the mail slot with your names on the envelopes. I look forward to seeing you tomorrow. Later tonight, my brother Todd will be working on the grounds and getting decorations set up for our Halloween festivities. Please let him know if you need anything.

Lucas

"I can honestly say this is the first time I have ever checked myself into a bed-and-breakfast," Tina giggled.

Nikki grabbed the wine and glasses. "This is what I'm talkin' about!"

"Let's drop our bags in our rooms and then explore the house before we go to the Cantina. It could give us a leg up for the dinner theater tomorrow if we know the layout of the house."

"Trish, that is a great idea! You are always plotting for the win. Speaking of wins, how did your pitch to Sylvie go?"

Now was as good a time as any to tell them I no longer worked for Palm Pointe. We talked as we explored the beautiful old mansion.

"Um. Not as well as I had hoped. She wasn't interested in the debut author I found."

"I'm so sorry. You mentioned you thought it would be a hard sell, that she prefers to work with already established authors."

I chewed my bottom lip and nodded.

"Trish, what did you do?" asked Nikki.

"I, er, well, she turned down the pitch before I even told her the plot of the book. Then she asked what I was thinking."

"Oh no!" Nikki and Tina said at the same time. I could tell they were trying to stifle a giggle.

"Did she fire you?" Tina asked.

I nodded. "It's all good. We all know that I need to work for myself. This face and mouth can't have a boss."

Tina looked at me, concern etched across her face. "What's the plan now, Trish?"

"I've been squirreling away funds for a rainy day. I'm going to work on my novel through the end of the year. It should be ready to publish early next year. There are a couple of magazines that buy articles from me regularly and, depending on how much the novel brings in, I should be able to write full-time. If I'm not bringing in enough between the magazines and my novel, I can always work at the bookstore. Now let's get back to exploring!"

Nikki and Tina still looked concerned, but I marched into the hallway, determined to drop the topic of losing my job.

"Guys, look at this grandfather clock. It's huge. I bet I could fit inside." Nikki opened the door and discovered a secret passage.

"Ohmygosh! That is so cool! Let's see where it goes. I bet there are more hidden doorways. You know they'll use these during the mystery dinner. It would be a terrible waste if they don't."

"It might be fun to see if we can find other entrances from the outside before exploring the passage."

"I love that idea, Trish!" Tina sprinted up the stairs. "Like this antique wardrobe, it could totally be an entrance." She pulled open the doors and moved aside the coats that hung inside. "Or not."

"Ooh, look at this full-length mirror. It could be another way into the secret passages." I pushed the mirror to the side, revealing a dark hallway.

"Okay, guys, at first finding secret passages was exciting, but now I am concerned there might be entrances in our rooms."

"Nikki, your job has really given you quite the imagination." I laughed.

"Maybe, but I'd still feel better if we checked our rooms."

Tina and I shook our heads but agreed that it couldn't hurt to look. We returned to the hall outside our rooms. "Whose room should we check first?" I asked.

"Mine. I noticed a mini bar earlier. I'm going to pour myself a drink."

"Of course you are, Nikki," I said with a chuckle.

"Do either of you want anything?"

"Yes. I'd love a cosmopolitan."

"Tina, I'm not a freaking bartender." Nikki grabbed two bottles from the fridge. "You can have beer or wine."

Tina laughed. "Wine."

"What do you say?" Nikki said in a sing-songy voice.

Tina threw a pillow at Nikki. "Please."

Tina and I thoroughly checked the room while Nikki poured the drinks. We didn't find any hidden doors in Nikki's room.

"Well, that's a relief," Nikki said. "Let's check the other two rooms."

Thankfully, we didn't find anything of concern in either Tina's or my rooms. But I was suitably jealous of the enormous bookcase in Tina's room.

"Guys, we better get some food in Tina before these drinks go to her head."

"What? You think just because I'm married with children that I can't hold my alcohol anymore? Come on, Nikki, you know me better than that." And she promptly tripped over the cedar chest at the foot of my bed.

"Riiight. You obviously still have the same tolerance you had in college. Lightweight." Nikki laughed.

"Let's order a ride and head to the Cantina." I looked at my phone. "I don't have a signal. Do either of you?"

Nikki and Tina looked at their phones.

"I do." Tina raised her phone.

While we waited for our ride, I told Nikki and Tina the legend of Captain Sterling.

"That is a fascinating story! Are there really holes dug every year?" Tina asked.

I shrugged. "I don't know. I only recently heard the story."

Nikki rolled her eyes. "Of course not. It's just a ruse for the tourists."

When we returned a few hours and a couple of margaritas later, the house was dark. We flipped the light switch, but the lights didn't turn on.

"A fuse must have blown. I don't know where the fuse box is located. I'll call Lucas and ask him about it." I pulled out my phone but didn't have cell reception. "Do either of you have any cell reception?"

They both checked their phones only to see 'no signal' displayed in red.

"I noticed a phone on the desk when we checked in. I'll try that." I picked up the receiver, hearing nothing, I returned it to the cradle. "Phone is dead, too." I sighed. "I guess we need to find the fuse box."

I turned on my phone flashlight and rummaged in the drawers of the desk, hoping to find a real flashlight so we wouldn't run down the batteries on our phones. Finding one, I flipped it on and turned off the one on my phone.

"The most logical place for a fuse box is the basement," Nikki said, shaking her head. "I'm not looking forward to going down there in the dark."

"B-A-S-E-M-E-N-T" Tina clapped as she said each letter. "To the basement!" she yelled.

"Tina, we aren't cheering our team to victory. We are just looking for the fuse box."

Tina giggled. "I didn't even realize I did that. It's a habit. Cheering often helps motivate my twins when they don't want to help clean up their toys."

We hadn't toured the basement during our earlier exploration of the property. The wooden stairs creaked as we descended them. The basement was cool and damp, and it smelled musty. It was much larger than we expected, with naked lightbulbs hanging from the ceiling with strings to turn them on. Eventually, we found the fuse box.

"Here's the problem. There's a fuse missing."

"Nikki, you mean a breaker needs flipped, right?" I asked.

"No. This system hasn't been upgraded, and it still uses physical fuses. These old units are notorious for blowing fuses but not missing them."

"Someone intentionally took it out. Why would they do that?" I asked.

"One probably blew, and they took it out to replace it, but discovered they didn't have extras down here. Let's look around. If we don't find any here, we can look in the office area."

I started searching the cupboards near the fuse box. Not finding any, we headed upstairs. We searched the office but didn't find replacement fuses there either. I shrugged. "Not much to be done about it tonight, I guess."

Tina started bouncing on the balls of her feet. "Let's light a fire in the library. We can talk by the fire, maybe even tell some Halloween ghost stories!"

"Your enthusiasm is contagious, Tina. Let's do it. But first, these heels have got to go! My feet are killing me."

We placed our shoes by the front door and padded into the library barefoot.

Tina knelt in front of the fireplace. "Good news, guys. This is a gas fireplace." She turned the nozzle and fire sprouted from the fake logs.

"It's odd that they upgraded the fireplace and not the electrical," Nikki mused as she headed for one of the chairs circling the fireplace.

Nikki stopped suddenly in front of me, causing me to bump into her. "Yo, Nik, keep it moving." I laughed.

"Um, guys?"

I peered over Nikki's shoulder to see what she was looking at. There was a man slouched in the recliner in front of her. There was a reddish-brown stain next to him on the headrest. "Is...is that blood?" I asked.

"This is the ultimate buzz kill," Nikki said as she approached the man. She touched his arm, and it flopped off the armrest. Her eyes were wide as she placed her fingers on his neck to check his pulse. She shook her head and moved her hand under his nose. "I don't feel a pulse or detect any breathing. I think he's dead."

"Did they start the mystery early?" Tina looked around the room and was almost giddy with excitement.

I joined Nikki by the man, who looked a lot like Lucas. I pulled my leather gloves out of my jacket and adjusted his head with a gloved hand. There was a large bloody gash on his head. "Uh, I…I don't think so. I think he is actually dead." Just then, there was a loud crash as we heard someone run through the house and a door slammed shut.

Tina and I screamed.

Nikki grumbled, "Still want to tell ghost stories, Tina?"

I walked to the phone on the table and lifted the receiver. It was still dead. I checked my phone and had one bar of signal. "I don't know how long I'll have a signal. I'll call Lucas. He lives in the old servants' quarters on the edge of the property. He can get here faster than the police." The call rang through to his voicemail. "Uh, Lucas, this is Trish. When we returned from dinner, the power was out and we just found an unconscious, possibly dead man. I believe might be Todd in the library." I went to disconnect the call, "Oh shoot! I lost the signal somewhere during the message."

"Trish! Really? That is the message you left?"

"What was I supposed to say, Nikki? 'Hey Lucas, we ran into a snafu. Could you call me at your earliest convenience?'"

Nikki shook her head. "I should have made the call."

Tina patted my shoulder. "Don't worry about it, Trish. It's done now."

"Should we walk over to his place?" Nikki asked.

I shook my head. "I don't know for sure where it is. It's probably better if we don't go traipsing around in the dark."

"I guess we are on our own." Nikki looked around the room. "I think we should try to figure out what happened. We'll start in here and, hopefully, we will find something that will tell us what to do next."

Tina looked around the room nervously. "Do you really think we should? I mean, wouldn't we be contaminating the scene or something? It's not like we're trained investigators."

"Well, I can't just sit around waiting for Lucas and the police to get here. We don't even know when Trish's phone lost the signal. Lucas might not get any message at all. We'll be careful to not disturb anything, and we can wear our gloves."

We turned on our flashlights and started looking around the body first, then worked our way out looking for clues.

There was a loud clang, then Nikki said, "I just stumbled on the murder weapon."

"Nik, where are you?"

"I tripped on a shovel and fell. I am stuck between the wall and the couch with the stupid thing."

"Don't touch it! It's evidence."

"Thank you, Captain Obvious. And it's too late; I fell on the blooming thing. So far, I have managed to not put my hands on it. To keep it that way, Trish, I'm going to need you to help me up."

"Let me. I'm closer."

"No way, Tina. You have kids. I am not risking your prints being on here."

"What am I? Disposable?" I joked.

I helped Nikki extract herself from behind the couch. As the flashlight glinted on the wall, I noticed a blood spatter pattern. "Hmm. That's weird."

"What's weird?" Tina asked.

"See the blood spatter by the shovel? If he was hit while sitting in the chair, there should be spattering there, but I don't recall seeing any. We should look again."

"Trish, you're right! There is a big pool of blood behind his head where it was resting on the chair, but there are no smaller drops anywhere around."

"That means he was moved to the chair after he was hit. This would be easier if there were more light," I said, my voice shrill.

As if in answer to a prayer, the library suddenly lit up, as did the adjacent rooms.

"Thank goodness!" Tina and I exclaimed in unison.

"Uh, guys, that's not good!"

"We have light. Why isn't that good, Nik?"

"Because there was a fuse missing, remember? If everything suddenly turned back on, there's someone here with us. They weren't leaving when we heard the door slam. Trish, try the phone."

Unfortunately, the landline was still dead, and our cells were not getting a signal.

"Okay, we can't just sit here. We need a plan. Obviously, we stay together. What else? Tina, Nikki, do either of you have other suggestions?"

"Let's start by the shovel. Maybe now that the power is on, we might be able to see clues in the blood spatter."

"I agree with Nikki. That seems like the best place to start."

I looked toward the library door. "Should one of us stand watch or something?"

Nikki shook her head, "No way! We stay close together."

The shovel had clearly been thrown behind the couch, but a few paces to the left there were more bloodstains on the wall. They started at about four feet high and extended up to about seven feet.

"I think he was hit here. Look, there is a sort of person shaped spot on the wall that is clear of blood and there are muddy footprints on the floor." The prints led to the chair where the body sat.

"Well, I guess we should look around the body for more clues."

DONG...DONG...DONG...

The grandfather clock rang ten times.

We walked in a tight circle toward the man. With the light now on in the room, we could see footprints clearly, all of them muddy and some mixed with blood. There was also blood on his fingertips as if he had reached back to feel his head after he was hit. I looked at his boots and the prints on the floor.

"Guys, look at his shoes. The prints and boots are pretty close, but these shoes are very worn. I don't think they would leave such sharp impressions."

Nikki leaned down for a closer look. "I think you're right. It appears the shoes that left the marks are the same brand, and at least close to the same size, but I don't think they were left by the deceased."

"So, um, if there is only one set of prints..." My voice cracked and I cleared my throat. "Does that mean someone was strong enough to carry him to the chair?"

Tina shrugged. "Let's not worry about it. We already knew someone else was here. The strength of that person changes nothing. So, follow the footprints!" Tina twirled her index finger in the universal 'let's move' sign.

We followed the prints out of the library.

THUMP! THUMP!

We stopped short, hearing the rhythmic banging at the top of the stairs. We ran up the stairs and discovered a window open; the wind causing the curtains to flutter and the frames to bounce back against the house. Honestly, I was surprised the window pane hadn't broken. I reached out and grabbed the window frame, pulled it closed, and latched the lock.

"Do you think the murderer went out the window?" I asked.

Tina shook her head and Nikki answered, "No. I think they were trying to direct us away from something else. Unless there is a trellis or a tree right out the window, I doubt anyone would risk trying to escape that way."

"Good point."

"OOOH! Guys, the secret passages."

"Tina, I'm not sure I am ready to venture into those just yet," I said. But as I turned around, I backed into the mirror at the top of the stairs.

"Fudgesticks! The tracks end in front of the mirror."

"Fudgesticks, Tina?"

"What? I'm a mom now." She gestured toward the mirror. "After you."

Nikki and I looked at each other. She sighed, "Rock, paper, scissors?"

"You really want to determine who enters first with a game?" I asked.

Nikki lifted her left fist. I shrugged and did the same. In the first three rounds, we both made the same symbol. On the fourth round, I held my fingers in the scissors sign, and she made the rock sign.

"I guess it's me." Turning on the flashlight, I pushed aside the mirror and entered. Nikki and Tina followed close behind me, each of them with a hand on the shoulder of the person in front. "Huh. I really thought there would be more cobwebs in here."

"That means we're on the right track!" Tina sounded delighted with the discovery.

"Tina, I'm not sure I want to be on the right track."

"Come on, Trish! We came here for a murder mystery. Embrace the opportunity!"

I shook my head. "Tina, the plan was to investigate a fake murder, not a real one!"

"Potato, patato."

"I don't think that applies to this situation."

We approached a fork in the secret passage. "Which way should we go?"

Nikki looked down both hallways. "Take the left. The right path still has spider webs hanging across."

We turned left and followed it a few steps. Up ahead, light was streaming in from a slightly open door. We pushed it open and found ourselves in Tina's room. Her belongings were ransacked and discarded around the room.

Nikki stood by the open bookcase, feeling the edges for a latch. "Of course, there is an entrance to the secret passages behind the bookcase. I can't believe I missed this earlier."

"I can. You were pretty focused on the contents of your glass," Tina laughed.

"Is anything missing?" I asked.

"My purse has been with me since we left for the restaurant. The worst they could take is clothes and toiletries. Let's leave the room as it is. When the police get here, they can go over the room for prints. Whoever did this isn't here anymore. Let's go into the hallway and see if we can find any clues where they went."

"Okay, but you're not sleeping in here!"

Tina and Nikki laughed. "Trish, I don't think any of us will be sleeping tonight."

My face flushed. "Valid point."

"Trish?"

We all jumped at the sound of a man's voice.

"Trish, are you here?"

Recognizing the voice, I called out, "Lucas, we're upstairs." I darted down the hallway and met Lucas at the top of the stairs.

"What are you doing upstairs?"

I shrugged. "Following leads."

Lucas slapped his forehead. "You guys should have left! What if the murderer is still here?"

Tina, Nikki, and I looked at each other and broke out in nervous chuckles.

"Uh, confession time. They are, or at least they were."

"Trish! Why didn't you leave?"

"Did you see a car outside? The landline is dead, and we haven't been able to get a signal on our cells long enough to order a rideshare. Besides, if I'm being honest, leaving didn't occur to me."

"Trish, you haven't changed a bit." Lucas shook his head. "Chief Robins should be here shortly. Why don't you walk me through what happened tonight?"

"The night has already been pretty draining. I'd rather only recount what happened once. Can we wait until the chief arrives?"

Nikki lifted her hand to shake Lucas's. "Nikki, and this is Tina. How do you know Trish?"

"Oh, my gosh! I am so sorry. I should have introduced everyone right away. Lucas was my lab partner in chem freshman year."

Nikki shook her head, "Honey, you wouldn't remember introductions in the best of times, and these are not, um, normal circumstances."

The front door banged open. "Hello?"

We followed Lucas down the stairs. "Chief Robins, thank you for coming so quickly. This is Trish, Nikki, and Tina. Ladies, Chief Robins."

"Well, show me what is so important you had to drag me out on my night off," the chief grunted.

I had expected the chief to be an overweight middle-aged man, but he was a muscular man in his early thirties. He clearly worked out, often. His worn Levi's hugged his hips in all the right places. At least I could enjoy a little eye candy while we talked about murder.

"We found a body. A dead body." Tina interjected.

"Are you sure it's my brother?"

I shook my head. "I've never met Todd, so I can't be sure, but he looks a lot like you."

Lucas nodded grimly and seemed to brace himself as I led him and Chief Robins into the library and pointed toward the recliner. "The body is in the chair and there is a bloody shovel behind the couch."

Nikki looked uncomfortable with Chief Robins, but I couldn't figure out why. She nudged me and looked down at his shoes. They were caked with mud that he was tracking all over the room.

Ah! Nikki has always hated inept authority figures.

I glanced at the prints Robins left, and they looked remarkably like the ones by Lucas's body. "Uh, Chief, your boots are pretty muddy. It is probably best if you put on some of those blue booties, so we don't mess up the evidence."

"I know how to run a crime scene! You don't have to tell me things you learned from watching crime shows on TV," he bellowed. He looked down at his boots. "I don't have any foot coverings in my car. I'll just take my shoes off. Lucas, would you mind putting them by the door for me?"

Lucas took a step back and dropped into the chair opposite the recliner. He ran his hand over his face, his eyes glassy and unfocused as the chief removed his boots.

"I'll take care of them," Nikki said quickly. "Lucas should stay. It's his brother after all."

As Nikki left the room, Chief Robins began taking pictures of the room.

Nikki took the shoes and turned right at the doorway, instead of setting them on the mat to the left. When she returned, she set the boots on the mat while stuffing a baggie into her jeans pocket.

"So, tell me how you ladies came across Todd's body."

Nikki recounted the events of the night for Lucas and Chief Robins, beginning with finding the electricity out, discovering the body, and ending with finding Tina's room ransacked. She told him about everything we did, except our tour of the hidden hallways.

Lucas stood and walked over to the phone. He lifted and re-placed the receiver. Then he checked the cord and found it was disconnected from the wall. He plugged it in and lifted the receiver again. The beautiful sound of a loud dial tone now emanated from it. Lucas looked at the chief. "I need to call my sister. Do you want to call Gary at the morgue first?"

I slapped my forehead. "I didn't even think to check the cord."

"I need to take some pictures and examine the scene, but I should be able to get that done before he gets here. Call him for me, would you?" Robins snapped a few pictures of Todd and the bloodstain at different angles. He seemed to hesitate, then he walked closer and moved Todd's head to the side. He took some shots of the stain on the chair and the wound on Todd's head.

"Not to tell you how to do your job, but shouldn't you be wearing gloves?" Nikki asked.

"Usually, yes, but the scene has already been contaminated by you ladies, so it doesn't really matter, does it?" he grumbled.

"Actually, other than checking for his pulse, we wore gloves when we touched him or anything in the room, after we discovered him, that is." I waved the gloves, still clenched in my hands.

"I guess we learned something from TV crime shows after all," Nikki snapped, glaring at the chief.

Tina and I shook our heads while stifling giggles.

Robins angrily put on gloves as he walked back over to the shovel. "Is this where you found it?"

"Yes. We didn't touch it, other than Nikki falling on it." I pointed to the wall near the couch. "We believe Todd was standing here when he was hit, and the person that hit him threw the shovel behind the couch before moving the body to the chair."

"Do you want a gold star for being such observant junior detectives?" Robins snarked. He took a few more pictures of the red pattern dotting the wall, focusing on the empty space.

Forget the eye candy. His personality was all Sour Patch Kids.

DONG...DONG...DONG...DONG...

The clock announced another hour had passed, eleven o'clock.

Gary arrived and loaded Todd into the van.

Lucas turned to Gary. "I'll meet you at the morgue."

"Lucas, I can't have you in the room while I examine Todd."

"I understand. I'll watch from the window."

"I'm going to head back to the station myself."

"Um, Chief, what about Tina's room? Shouldn't you look at that, since someone ransacked it?" I asked.

Lucas glanced at Chief Robins. He seemed to be curious about the answer as well.

"I don't see how that could be related."

"Of course it's related! We are the only ones staying at the manor tonight," I snapped.

"It was probably just some teens pulling early Halloween pranks."

"I don't buy that," I said. "If that were true, wouldn't our other rooms have been disturbed too? And wouldn't there be toilet paper in trees, smashed pumpkins, or something?"

"You're probably right, Chief," Tina interjected, smiling sweetly.

"It's about time someone gave me credit for knowing my job." After shoving his feet into his boots, Robins stomped out the door.

Nikki watched out the window until she could no longer see the chief's headlights.

"Guys, I think there was blood on his shoes. I brought his boots to the kitchen and took pictures of the size and soles of the chief's boots and scraped a mud sample from them into this baggie." She handed me the baggie and walked over to the prints on the floor, then took a second baggie from her pocket and picked up the letter opener from the desk. She crouched down and scraped some mud from the floor into the baggie.

As I watched Nikki collect the sample, I noticed a glint under the desk.

Nikki stood up with the baggies in hand. "Does anyone have a pen?"

Tina pulled a pen from her purse and labeled each of the baggies. Nikki put both baggies in her pocket.

I leaned down to see what caused the glint. "Guys! There is a cell phone under the desk!" I plucked a tissue from the box on the desk and picked up the phone. "What should I do with this?"

"Give it to Lucas the next time you see him. It's probably Todd's phone," Tina replied.

Nikki nodded in agreement and then took out her phone and opened the photo gallery. She scrutinized the tread of the prints and the pictures she took. "The tread looks the same, but there is no way to know if the chief wears the same size shoes as the murderer."

"So, what do we do now?" I asked.

"We go to Tina's room and see if anything is missing and look for clues in there."

"Guys, I'm sure that nothing is missing, unless whoever tossed my room is into granny panties."

"I thought you wore designer thongs," I joked.

Tina laughed. "That was before I had kids. Now I'm all about comfort."

"At the very least, we'll help you get everything put away," I said.

Tina and I entered her room while Nikki slipped into her room. She returned a minute later carrying three glasses and a bottle of wine. "I don't know about you girls, but I could use a drink. The margaritas wore off a long time ago."

The clock struck twelve while Nikki poured the wine. We picked up Tina's belongings and the books that were scattered on the floor. Noticing that one book had a page turned down, I opened it to the page and found a map crudely drawn in the margins, complete with an 'X' in the corner. "Guys! I think whoever tossed the room was looking for this."

We sat on the foot of the bed and looked at the small etchings.

Nikki scrutinized the drawing. "I bet these are latitude and longitude numbers."

"Ooooh! Guys, 'X' marks the spot! Could this be a copy of the map that Captain Sterling made when he buried his treasure? We should try to find the long-sought-after fortune! We came for an adventure, after all."

"Tina, don't you think we had enough adventure already?"

"Trish, don't be a downer. Besides, it might help us figure out who killed Todd. I don't think Chief Robins could find a pumpkin in the proverbial patch, let alone a murderer. Lucas told him that Todd was dead, and he didn't even bring anything to collect evidence. Even I noticed, he didn't take a sample of the mud on the floor."

"Let's just say it is a treasure map, and that the latitude and longitude numbers coordinate with the 'X.' How will we possibly figure it out? We can't get a signal on our phones for more than a couple of minutes at a time. Since Beaubien Manor has been closed most of the year, I doubt they have Wi-Fi here."

"Do you think they still have dial-up?" asked Nikki, grinning.

"Nikki, dial-up is so last century," I laughed.

"For most of the nation, yes. But rural areas took a lot longer to have access to high-speed internet. My brother just upgraded his system last year."

Tina was bouncing on her feet again. "Nikki, that's a fabulous idea!"

"Let me grab my laptop. I'll meet you at the front desk."

Nikki set her laptop on the counter, unplugged the phone, and clicked it into an adapter on her computer. We heard screeching and whirring as the internet connected. She opened the browser, and we watched the page load very, very slowly. My parents used to joke about how slow the internet used to be. Their descriptions paled to the reality of dial-up. Nikki typed in the latitude and longitude that was scribbled in the book, into Google Earth, then she zoomed in.

"It seems like the spot would be out there by the plastic gravestones. While we have internet, I want to research Chief Robins. Something about him raises the hair on the back of my neck. Following my intuition makes me a successful bounty hunter." She blew on her fingernails and rubbed them across her chest.

"At least you're humble," I joked.

Nikki typed in "Juniper Beach, SC, police chief." The site displayed a picture of a slightly younger Chief Robins.

Nikki summarized what she found. "Sterling Robins was appointed to the position of Chief of Police by the mayor. Sterling is the son of Marge (Sterling) and Frank Robins." Nikki gasped. "Guys! What was the name of that pirate in the local legend?"

"Swedish fish! It was Captain Sterling! Do you think they are related?"

"Tina, we need to re-teach how you to properly swear." Nikki shook her head. "Let's see if we can find out." She returned to the search engine and typed "Captain Sterling."

The results mostly recounted the local stories. We learned that Captain Sterling and his mistress had a baby. They later married, he gave up the seas and moved to the area.

"Nikki, do you have an account with a genealogy site?"

"That's a good idea, Tina. But let's start with social media. Often when someone has a connection to famous people, they mention it in their bio. One of my bounties claimed she was the 16th great-granddaughter of Pocahontas," she chuckled.

Nikki pulled up her Facebook account and searched for Marge Robins. There were a couple dozen profiles with that name, so we narrowed the search by location. Finding the right Marge Robins, we read her bio. She indeed claimed to be a descendant of Captain Sterling. She even joked about wanting to find the missing treasure before she died.

I continued reading her page. "Oh, guys. She died last month after a long battle with cancer."

"Um, I think we may have found a motive... assuming Chief Robins is the one that murdered Todd."

"That's quite the leap, Nikki."

"That's true, Tina. But I got the feeling that he knows proper police protocol; he just wasn't following it. We all saw him touch Todd without gloves, so later, when his DNA is on the body, he has a plausible explanation. No self-respecting law enforcement would ever wear muddy boots into a crime scene." Nikki ticked her fingers as she spoke. "He didn't get fingerprints from anything in the room. Did you notice he didn't even take the weapon into evidence? Then, let's not forget that he didn't want to investigate Tina's ransacked room." Nikki rubbed her forehead.

"What are you thinking, Nikki?" I asked.

"I wish I had brought my kit. I'd love to get the prints off the shovel."

"I wish I believed he neglected getting prints and taking the shovel because he isn't used to major crimes in this area." I sighed.

"What do you need, Nikki?" Tina interrupted me. "Chief Robins should have done that, but he didn't even bag the shovel and take it into evidence."

"Um, a fine powder, a brush, some clear tape and paper."

"Will this work?" Tina held up her blush, some tape, and a mini notebook.

"You carry Scotch tape in your purse?"

"Trish, when you are a mom, you can judge the contents of my purse. Until then, SHHH!"

"I'm not sure if it will work, but it's worth a try. Are you okay with me ruining your blush?"

"We found a body in the library, and you're concerned about wasting makeup? Use the blush!"

Nikki jabbed at the makeup with the brush until it was a fine, loose powder and lightly dusted it on the shovel handle, then she gently blew the excess blush powder off. On the handle, we could see a few prints. Most were just partial, but there were two that looked complete. Nikki placed a strip of tape over each of them, pulled the tape up, and stuck them both to a piece of paper. She handed everything to Tina. Tina carefully placed everything in her purse.

BANG!

We looked at each other in surprise.

"Was...was that a gunshot?" I stuttered.

Nikki chuckled, "Trish, I think that was a car backfiring."

Tina ran to the window and looked outside. "The chief's car is back."

Nikki walked to the door and threw it open. "Oh hey, Chief! Did you need something else?"

Chief Robins looked startled; a bead of perspiration was visible on his temple. "Oh, hello, ladies. I, er, um, I'm glad you're still here. I thought you might have decided to get a room in town, what with the murder and all. I have a couple more questions if you don't mind."

"Of course! Anything we can do to help figure out what happened to Todd." Nikki waved her hand behind the door.

I ran over to her laptop, closed the lid, and unplugged it from the phone line. I was just plugging the phone back in as Robins entered the room.

I stood in front of the desk, blocking his view of the laptop. "What did you want to ask us, Chief?"

A deer could not compete with the 'trapped in the headlights' look that the chief wore. "Oh, er, um," He pulled his notebook from his front pocket and flipped through a few pages. "I wanted to confirm the time that you arrived back from your dinner."

"Eight-thirty," we said in unison.

"Right. Right. And did any of you know Todd Beaubien?"

"No. Lucas and I were lab partners in college. We didn't know each other outside of class really. I didn't even know he had a brother until we signed up for the Halloween mystery party," I explained.

"Isn't that scheduled for tomorrow?"

DONG!

One o'clock. I was beginning to really hate that clock.

"It is. We wanted to spend some time together before the festivities, so we came a day early."

"Could you excuse me? I need to use the restroom." Nikki nodded toward her computer and headed out of the room.

The chief raised his eyebrows. "She sneak off often?"

Tina and I looked at each other. Was he seriously trying to implicate Nikki?

Tina cleared her throat. "I'm sure you're not implying what it sounds like. The three of us have been together since we returned from dinner. That was hours ago. Her needing the restroom doesn't seem odd to me. In fact, my bladder isn't what it was before I had children. Could you excuse me as well?"

I glanced behind me and noticed that the door on the grandfather clock was slightly ajar. I walked around Robins and stepped toward the door. "Is there anything else we can do for you, Chief Robins?"

"Uh, no. I think that is everything."

Tina returned a couple of seconds later.

"The other one is sure taking a while."

"We ate at the Cantina. Mexican food never sits well with Nikki. Not that she would ever admit that." I laughed and winked at Tina.

Tina shook Robins's hand. "Well, good night, Chief."

"Um, I don't think you ladies should stay here tonight."

"Thank you for your concern, Chief Robins. We'll be fine. Have a good night."

I walked the chief to the door. As I reached for the knob, the door opened and Lucas walked in, followed by a woman I didn't recognize.

"Lucas, I feel just awful for you!" I gave Lucas a hug and slipped the phone we found into his back pocket as I whispered, "I think this is Todd's phone. I'm not sure we can trust Chief Robins."

The woman raised her eyebrows as she watched me slip the phone into his pocket.

"What's going on here, Lucas?" asked Chief Robins.

"This is my sister, Andrea. She just arrived in town and wanted to go over what happened to Todd."

"I've got it under control."

"Of course you do, Chief. I'm sure you can appreciate that I want to see the scene of our brother's murder." She flipped open a black wallet and showed him her FBI badge. "Unofficially, of course."

"Oh, I'm sorry. My mind feels like it is slogging through mud ever since I learned of Todd's death. I should have mentioned that Andrea works for the FBI," Lucas said.

Chief Robins gulped. "Well, I am happy to share my notes. Has Gary wrapped up his preliminary findings already?"

"I don't know. Andrea called to tell me she had arrived in town. She wanted to come over right away, so I didn't make it to the morgue," Lucas answered.

Andrea took the notebook from Robins and flipped through the pages. She nodded a couple of times and made some notes in her own book. She handed the notebook back to Robins. "Thank you, Chief. That was very helpful. Ladies, could you walk me through the events of the night in your own words?"

"Of course. Should we go into the library where we found Todd?"

Nikki was descending the stairs as we walked to the library. "Oh, Chief! You're still here. I am so sorry about running off like that. I guess those fish tacos didn't sit well tonight." She turned to Andrea and extended her hand. "Hello. My name is Nikki."

Andrea shook her hand. "Andrea. Lucas and Todd are my brothers."

Andrea was the first person to walk into the library. She put on gloves and foot coverings. "The shovel is still here? Shouldn't you have bagged it and taken it in to be processed, Chief?"

"I, er, um, yes. I didn't have anything with me earlier and didn't want to risk destroying evidence."

Chief Robins walked over to the shovel. "What is this powder all over the handle?"

Tina, Nikki, and I looked at each other. I shrugged. "We uh, well, you didn't take the shovel and, uh, we, uh, we decided to try to learn what we could about this, um, situation." The more I talked, the more annoyed Chief Robins looked.

"What did you do?" He snarled; a vein bulged on his forehead.

"We dusted the handle for fingerprints?"

"What do you think this is? A Scooby Doo episode?" He gave an aggravated growl. Taking a deep breath, he continued, "What did you use?"

"Blush," we said in unison. Tina reached into her purse; Nikki gave an almost imperceptible shake of her head. Tina tore a page from her notebook and gave it to the chief. "This is what we were able to pull from the handle."

"Did you know that Chief Robins is a descendant of Captain Sterling?" Nikki asked, pulling everyone's focus away from Tina's notebook.

"I'm not sure what that has to do with the murder," Robins grumbled.

"I just thought it was an interesting tidbit seeing how Todd was murdered on the property where legend says Captain Sterling buried his treasure. Isn't there something in the lore about a murder every fifty years?"

"If you believe in that kind of garbage."

"I find legends are often based on facts and have more to do with the present than we give them credit for. Wouldn't you agree, Chief?" asked Andrea. "Chief! Where are your booties?"

"No need really. I was in here earlier."

"Surely you were wearing shoe covers then?"

"I, er, I took my boots off by the door."

"After we pointed out that he should wear shoe covers," Nikki interjected.

While we talked to Andrea and Chief Robins, Lucas stood in the library doorway looking at Todd's phone. He pulled out his own phone and appeared to send a text message.

"These three think that they are experts on crime scenes because they've watched a few crime shows on TV," Chief Robins snapped and turned to leave the room. "If you need me, I'll be at the station."

Lucas followed Chief Robins to the front door. "Before you go Chief, I have a couple of things I want to discuss with you."

Lucas and Robins stood in the front entrance talking.

Andrea gave us an incredulous look.

"Is he always like that?" Andrea asked.

I shrugged. "We only just met him tonight, but in my limited experience..." I nodded.

"He is a narcissist, and not as incompetent as he acts. It seems like he's hiding something," Nikki added.

Andrea nodded. "I wish I had access to that fingerprint."

"The way he shoved it in his pants pocket, I don't know how usable it will be." I grimaced.

"Right. Lucas filled me in on what you told Robins earlier, and I looked at the chief's notes. Considering how he seems to be handling things, I'd love to know your thoughts."

"If I were playing a game of Clue, I'd bet the game that I know who, what, and where."

"Tell me what you're thinking, Trish."

"Continuing the Clue analogy, Chief Robins killed Todd in the library with the shovel."

Nikki took a breath and looked at me. I nodded, and she continued. "We, uh, we suspect Robins is the murderer or is covering up for the murderer, but we don't have proof."

Nikki led Andrea to the prints on the floor. They knelt down to examine them.

"We looked at Todd's boots and they seem to be the same pattern, but I don't think it was his boots that left the tracks. First, there was no mud on his boots, but also his tread was very worn. These imprints are much sharper than his boots would have made." Nikki pulled out her phone and showed Andrea the pictures of Robins's boots. "The chief was wearing a size eleven of the same brand of shoes as Todd. Unfortunately, I have no idea what size the prints are." Nikki stood up and pulled the baggies from her pocket. "We took samples of the mud from the floor and from Robins's shoes." She handed the baggies to Andrea.

"This is very helpful. Is there anything else you can tell me?"

Tina reached into her purse. "Um, is it obstruction of justice if we only gave Robins one of the prints we pulled?"

Andrea chuckled. "Robins wasn't joking about you three watching crime shows." She reached for the print. "I already shared this with Lucas, but Todd called me earlier tonight. He found some newly dug holes near where he set up the gravestone decorations. He said he thought he knew who made them and would take care of it. I heard a thud as we ended the call."

"Do you think you heard the shovel hitting Todd?" Nikki asked.

"I don't think so. It sounded more like a door shutting."

She turned toward the doorway where Lucas and Robins stood. "Lucas, I think you and Chief Robins should join us," Andrea said.

As they walked toward us, another officer entered the house.

"Thank you for joining us, Deputy Stevens," Lucas said.

"Lucas, what did you learn from Todd's phone?" asked Andrea.

Chief Robins turned to leave.

Lucas placed a hand on his shoulder. "Chief, you should stay for this."

Robins reluctantly walked back into the library.

Lucas handed a phone to the deputy. "This is Todd's phone. The passcode is 1505. You should look at his most recent photos. There is also a recording I believe to be relevant."

The deputy scrolled through the pictures and played the recording.

"What are you doing here, Chief?"

"Oh, um, I noticed some holes out front. I thought I would fill them in for you."

"Funny, it looked like you were the one digging them earlier. Did you find what you were looking for, Sterling?"

"It's really too bad you saw that, Todd."

THWACK!

The deputy stopped the recording. "Chief Robins, you are under arrest for the murder of Todd Beaubien."

"What in tarnation?! Just because I dug some holes? You know I'm no murderer!" The vein on the chief's forehead pulsed rapidly. It looked ready to explode.

"The pictures on the victim's phone show you digging on his property, and this recording is pretty incriminating. We will continue investigating, of course, but there is plenty of evidence to take you into custody. I am confident that we will find your boots match the tracks on the floor and that your fingerprints will be a match for those on the handle."

As the deputy loaded the chief into the back of his car, Chief Robins yelled, "I'd be a rich man living on a beach in Mexico if it weren't for the three of you!"

I turned to Nikki and Tina. "I can't believe we solved an actual murder!"

"And you have a whole new story idea!" Tina giggled.

Bellamina Court

 **Bellamina** is a mystery author known for crafting whodunits that blend suspense with charm. Her novel, *Whispers in the Night*, introduces readers to strong, independent women who tackle life's mysteries with wit and resilience.

When she's not writing, she enjoys beachside relaxation.

A former stay-at-home mom of seven, Bellamina now shares her home with four dogs and three cats. When she's not writing, she enjoys beachside relaxation with a margarita in hand.

For updates and exclusive content, visit www.BellaminaCourt .com.

Chapter Three

Love, Lies, and Lavender

Kristen Elizabeth

Best Friend <3: I'll be driving in for the Halloween Parade!

Ellie: It's about damn time I see you! I'm sorry I missed your show :'(

Best Friend <3: You can't always see me perform. Besides, Ivy got the lead this last show. I call favoritism for blondes >:(

Ellie: Aggie...you're also blonde.

Best Friend <3: Semantics. However, everyone was super duper jealous of my amazing bouquet – yet again! IDK how you do it – you have the eyes of an angel or something for flowers and plants...all that jazz and so on.

Ellie: You deserve only the best and most eye-catching florals. Plus, I'm an expert for a reason lol

Best Friend <3: I knew I kept you around for a reason! Also...can you give me the scoop on Ivy's costume? Pwetty pwease? <3

Ellie: No can do, buckaroo. You know my rules. Plus, I'm still placing the finishing touches on your costume entry.

Best Friend <3: Ugh, well, I tried. Guess we'll just need to see who wins this year!

Ellie: Quit stalling and start driving! Can't wait <3

Best Friend <3: See you in a few hours! <3

Ellie chuckles as she sets her phone on the glass countertop centered in the middle of her floral shop. She takes in a deep breath, the scents of eucalyptus, rose, and peony settling into her bones and providing some much-needed comfort for the stressful day ahead. A small chirping sound catches her attention. "Ah, there you are, Buster. You hungry, boy?"

The bearded dragon scurries across a shelf on the wall and darts to the back area. Ellie follows her beloved pet towards the cold room where she keeps inventory and pet-related food items. Buster prances in place as he awaits the apple slices kept in a secure mini fridge. "I get it, hold on." Ellie laughs as she places a few slices into Buster's dish. A jingle from the front-of-house brings her back to work mode.

"Yoohoo! Elizabeth, dear!" the older woman's voice calls. Ellie sighs in exasperation.

"Mrs. Palmer," Ellie greets with a plastered smile, "So lovely to see you. And, once again, it's Elodie. How can I help you?"

Mrs. Palmer decked out in a modest orange and black pencil skirt and matching jacket, grins at Ellie. "Ah, of course it is. I always forget that unique name of yours – Elizabeth is so much easier. But I was hoping to catch you early for a small favor. I will pay of course!"

Ellie raises an eyebrow in question. "Sure thing. Does it have to do with that?" She points to the large shopping bag in Mrs. Palmer's right hand.

"Why, yes, it does! You are so smart, Elizabeth! You must've gotten that from your father."

"Right. So, what did you need?"

"Sorry, sorry!" Mrs. Palmer hauls the bag onto the glass countertop with a thunk. "This is my newest hat and I'd love it if you could work your magic on it. It must be Halloween Parade ready!" She fiddles with the bag and reveals a large hat box. She slides it to Ellie, "Well, go on and have a peek."

Ellie undoes the silk ribbon and opens the large box to reveal a beret sat atop white tissue paper. "It's a simple enough hat, Mrs. Palmer. Do you have an idea in mind for what you want?"

"A bird's nest, but make it, as you kids say, spooky." Mrs. Palmer looks giddy with herself. "I'd love for some roses, maybe black or dark red, and something dead-looking. Can't show up to the parade in my usual getup!"

Ellie huffs a chuckle. "Of course, Mrs. Palmer. I can work my magic, as you said, and have something done for you by tomorrow morning for pickup. Is that okay?"

Mrs. Palmer places her right hand over her heart, "Elizabeth, dear, this will be perfectly acceptable. I know you're on a time crunch with Ivy's costume. She let me know last week she was having hers delivered tonight, so I greatly appreciate it."

"Not a problem. And, Mrs. Palmer, my name is Elodie – like Melody without the 'M'. Please call me Ellie."

Mrs. Palmer waves her hand dismissively. "Yes, yes, sorry dear. It's just Elizabeth it's such a lovely name – it suits you much better."

"Sure, it does. Anything else you need?" Ellie boxes the hat back up and places it on a nearby workstation.

"No, that is all! Thank you so much, Ellie! See – getting better all ready!" Mrs. Palmer shoots another smile at Ellie before rushing out of the shop.

Ellie shakes her head at the elderly woman's antics and combs through her hair with her fingers, a nervous habit developed during her teen years. "What a headache."

The clatter of Ellie's vibrating phone has her looking at the screen. 'Dad' is flashing on the caller ID. "Long time no talk, stranger," she answers.

A raspy chuckle comes through the line before the screen lights up with her father's face, "My little Petunia, how are you doing? Getting things ready for the parade this week?"

"Yep. It's tomorrow, Dad. You should remember this. It wasn't so long ago that you and Margot lived in Whispering Pines."

"Yeah, yeah. You know I don't keep up with that stuff. How's the shop doing?"

Ellie looks around her shop – Petunia's Petals, affectionately named for her middle name and father's favorite flower – the bright-colored bouquets and bushels placed artfully throughout the space, ensuring a pleasant atmosphere for anyone shopping. "Great, actually. I have two designs featured in the costume contest this year. Ivy Blake-Ellis and Aggie – they're still battling it out at the New York City Ballet before you ask."

Her dad chuckles fondly, "They still haven't grown out of that competition I see. Can you tell me anything about the concepts?"

"You know my policy, Dad." She mocks locking up her mouth with a key. "My lips are sealed. Sorry not sorry!"

"That's how it should be, Petunia. Speaking of keeping things sealed, I've been working on some cases for fun."

Ellie's eyebrows shoot up in surprise. "And Margot is cool with that? Aren't you supposed to be retired from the force?"

"Margot encouraged me, much to my surprise as well. She could see me missing the excitement. Consulting keeps my brain working. You should see some of this stuff, we'd both be able to solve them with no problem!"

"Ah, yes, our dynamic duo days. I do miss them sometimes, but you know where my passion lies, Dad."

"I know, trust me. But if you ever need a bit of brain stimulus, I might be able to see if I can send a couple of cases your way."

"I'm sure the chain of command would love that, Dad. I left that side a while ago. How is the Sunshine State, besides your consulting?"

"Margot and I love the beach! Much different from the coastline at Whispering Pines – more tropical and very lovely. You'd get a kick out of the plant life – do you ever order tropical things?"

"All the time, Dad. Anything floral or foliage related I do consider for many things." A sudden crash from the back room pauses

Ellie mid-sentence. "I hate to cut this short, Dad, but it seems like Buster knocked something over in the back."

"Ah, no worries. Tell my dragon friend I'll visit him soon. Take care of yourself!" He waves to his only daughter.

"You too, Dad. Love you!" Ellie hangs up her cell phone, "Buster! You better hide or else I'm making Mrs. Palmer's hat with your butt in it!" she calls to the back room.

She can hear the slight pitter-patter of Buster's claws against the tile as he scampers to hide.

------◆O◆------

The deep timbre of the doorbell can be heard from outside the heavy wooden doors. Ellie stands holding a garment bag, observing the ostentatious carvings embedded in the wood, before being met with a stern-looking woman. "Hey Rosita. I'm here for Ivy. Is she here?"

"Yes, Miss Ivy is home. Please come in and I shall have her meet you in the tea room."

Ellie shuffles inside. "Thanks, Rosita. How are you and Carlos doing?"

Rosita's face slightly softens, "My boy is thriving in the big city. He will be visiting soon for the parade. He will be graduating college next year – the first in our family."

"That's great, Rosita. I'm glad to hear he's doing well." Ellie is led through the lavish home. They bypass the double staircase – wrought iron scaffolding creating an elaborate railing – and continue through to the tea room. It is a simple room with a small round table and chairs, perfect for hosting a guest or two. The walls are tastefully decorated with pastel paintings and shelves containing knick-knacks and books. Ellie places the garment bag onto the table to begin unwrapping Ivy's costume.

"Ellie! I'm so glad you could make it!" Ivy's cheery voice filters into the room.

"Hey, Ivy! It's not a problem at all. How are you doing?" Ellie asks.

Ivy clears her throat, "Sorry about that. I think I have a cold or something, so just be prepared in case you catch what I have. But I'm feeling so much happier now that you've arrived. Is it ready? Can I see it?" Ivy clasps her hands together in a pleading gesture.

Ellie chuckles, "Yeah, of course. I hope it lives up to the hype. If we need to fix anything at all, it can be done before you hit the stage – that's to ensure the freshest possible florals for any that might wilt between now and tomorrow."

"Ah, that sounds great! I've been looking forward to the contest so much this year. And you promise that there isn't any lavender involved?"

Ellie crosses her heart, "Cross my heart and hope to die. There is no lavender on this dress at all. To get the same look, I went for blue marvel salvia. I wouldn't put you at risk like that. So, are you ready?"

Ivy grins, white teeth sparkling in the cascading light. Ellie motions her over to the table where the dress lies. The costume is simple in design – a high-low dress with a sweetheart neckline and off-the-shoulder straps. The florals, however, provide an eye-catching cascade of lilac, purple, and indigo. Interspersed within the florals sits sage green foliage to provide depth and dimension in color. "Well, what do you think?"

Ivy, with hearts in her eyes, gently touches the costume. "Oh my god, Ellie, this is amazing!"

Ellie smiles in return, "Thanks, Ivy. I was hoping you'd like it. Now, you can go try it on and see if we need to make any alterations to the sizing. I can't wait to see it on you."

Ivy squeals in delight. "Drew! You need to come see this!" Her screech echoes through the mansion. Ellie winces at the volume.

A few seconds pass before a tall man enters the tea room with a stack of papers in hand. "Hey, Ellie. Ivy, please, my ears are so close to bleeding. I can only imagine that Ellie's gone deaf now."

Ivy laughs at her husband's comment and playfully smacks his chest. "Hush, you. Everyone is fine – I'm just so excited. I'm going to go try it on right now. I'll be right back!"

Ivy rushes out of the small room in a flurry of excitement. Drew watches her fondly, a loving smile ghosting his face. "You really love her, huh?" Ellie asks.

Drew flat-out grins at Ellie. "With all my heart and soul. She really is the light of my life. I can't imagine it without her. And thanks again for participating in our wedding. It looked amazing."

"No problem, Drew. It was my pleasure – and you guys looked great. How's everything been since returning from your Europe tour?"

"Well, business is coming together. I know Ivy's family was iffy with her marrying me, but so far, they seem impressed that I've been able to handle my own business and treat Ivy like a queen. We should be ready to go public within the next few months, so that will only mean more growth."

Ellie nods her head, "That's really nice, Drew. I'm proud of you guys – stick it to these old richies."

Drew laughs loudly. "That's the plan, Ellie."

"Attention, attention! The Whispering Pines Halloween Costume Contest Winner has arrived!" Ivy steps back into the room, a floral train cascading behind her. "What's the verdict, judges?"

"You look beautiful, love. Turn around, and let's see the dress in action."

Ivy turns and the dress follows like a waterfall. "The fit looks great," Ellie comments. "How do you feel? Everything good?"

"It's great, Ellie. You did such an amazing job. I can't wait to wear it in the contest tomorrow. Thank you so much!" She grabs Ellie into a quick hug before noticing the papers on the small table. "Is that them? Where is a pen? I'll sign right now before I forget."

Drew rummages around the room and finds a black ink pen. "Here you are, love. I've signed as well, so as soon as this is done, I can submit it to the insurance company and we are good to go."

Ivy grins at Drew. "Perfect! This just ensures that we will both be protected. I love you, Drew." The soft smile she gives her husband makes Ellie believe in fairy tales – perhaps she should leave so the couple can share in what looks to be a private moment.

The loud slam of a door interrupts the trio's interaction. "Drew! I'm home."

"I'm guessing that must be Lily," Ellie inquires.

"You'd be correct," Drew sighs in irritation, a hand running down his face. "She thinks, for whatever reason, that our house is now her house. I know she's your sister, Ivy, but we need some type of privacy."

"I know, I know, Drew. But she's having a rough time, and she's my twin sister. She's my best friend." Ivy pouts as she signs the final page of the document. "I get it though; I'll have a talk with her."

"Let's continue with the fitting and then I can get out of your hair – one less person in your home and all." Ellie directs Ivy to stand still so she can ensure all pieces of the dress are intact.

"Drew? Where are you – oh here you are! Oh, Ivy, and Ellie? What's going on?" Lily questions.

"Hey, Lily. I'm doing the costume contest this year, remember? Ellie made my costume! Isn't it great?" Ivy looks at an identical face to her own, hope evident in her eyes for approval.

Lily sidles up to Drew, clinging to his arm. Ellie notices that Drew visibly tenses but does not pull away at that moment. "I think it's nice. What is the theme? Did you even have one?"

Ivy nods her head, mindful of Ellie working on the dress. "Think midnight woodland fairy. Ellie has a headpiece for me as well that we will put in place tomorrow. It's going to look amazing. I really want to win this year!"

"You'll probably win again like the last three years. So, Drew, how was your day today?" Lily quickly dismisses her sister in favor of her twin's husband.

"It was fine, Lily. Hey, why don't you get us some tea? I think we're all pretty thirsty here." He delicately removes himself from Lily's embrace.

"Sure, sure. I won't be as bad of a host as Ivy here." Lily winks playfully at her sister. "Ellie, drink?"

"I'm okay, thank you, Lily. We're almost done with the fitting, so I'll be out of here soon."

Lily shrugs nonchalantly. "Suit yourself. I have a unique tea blend that's to die for."

As Lily leaves the room, Drew sags in relief. "Are you sure you don't want anything, Ellie? We got so caught up in the dress – I feel bad I didn't offer you something sooner," Ivy confirms.

"I'm good, Ivy, really. I think we're all done here. I will leave the dress with you, but I'll pop by a few minutes before the contest begins to double-check the florals are good to go and help you with your hair. Do you need anything else from me before I go?"

Ivy shakes her head, "No, you've been such a big help already. Thank you, yet again. I keep saying it, but I really am so thankful you made this happen."

Ellie smiles, "Like I told Drew before, it was my pleasure to assist. I'll see you guys tomorrow at the parade then?"

Drew shakes Ellie's hand. "We'll see you there. Thanks for stopping by. I'll walk you to the door."

As Drew walks Ellie to the front door, they pass by Lily holding a tray containing a tea set and homemade cookies. Ellie swears she caught the swiftest scent of lavender on her way out.

———◆O◆———

Ellie's door chimes as it opens slowly. "Knock, knock, Elizabeth!"

Ellie sighs internally – when will she ever get her name right? "Mrs. Palmer. You're right on time this morning. I have your hat right here."

Ellie slides the hat box across the glass as Mrs. Palmer walks to the counter. "Ah! I cannot wait to see it. You truly are the best, Elizabeth!"

"Mrs. Palmer, it's Elodie – again please call me Ellie. I hope you like it."

"Right, right." Mrs. Palmer waves her hand dismissively, "I will remember. It's just that –"

"Elizabeth suits me so well, yes. You've said it many times before, Mrs. Palmer," Ellie drawls.

Ellie watches Mrs. Palmer's gloved hand lift the lid of the box. She is dressed in a disheveled black tulle ballgown with zombified makeup donning her face and neck. "Very festive outfit, Mrs. Palmer. Are you entering into the contest this year?"

"Oh no, dear! I will be a judge, however. I'm much too old for these types of things. I'll let you youngsters have your fun."

Mrs. Palmer's eyes light up with joy upon seeing the hat. The once plain black beret is now a collection of twigs, dead rose petals, ashen eucalyptus, and a distressed fake bird. "This is perfect, Ellie! How much do I owe you?"

Ellie smiles at Mrs. Palmer's genuine happiness. "I'll email you the invoice. Worry about it after the parade – let's just have some fun."

Mrs. Palmer claps her hands together. "This is much appreciated!" She places the hat atop her mussed-up hairdo. "How do I look?"

"Spooky," Ellie chuckles. "I'm glad it fits your costume so well."

Buster takes this as his cue to run off from Ellie's shoulder and onto the counter. "Oh!" Mrs. Palmer places a hand over her heart. "You spooked me, Buster!" The bearded dragon simply lowers his head, a sign to both women that he is in dire need of attention in the form of head pats. "What a lovely lizard you are, Buster." Mrs. Palmer gently strokes atop his head, mindful of the scales and spikes.

"Thanks. He's the best assistant I could have around here." Ellie places the hat box to the side as Mrs. Palmer digs into her purse.

"I have to at least give you something before I join the festivities." She pulls out a hundred-dollar bill. "You can spend this today at the parade. All items are on me today, Ellie!"

Ellie points at her and smirks. "Getting better already! See you at the parade, Mrs. Palmer."

Mrs. Palmer waves as she exits the small shop. Ellie picks up the countertop, double-checking that everything is in place. She places Buster back on her shoulder and grabs a large black garment bag.

The atmosphere in the town square of Whispering Pines is whimsical. The main street of the tiny downtown has been transformed into a Halloween paradise. Pumpkins and scarecrows adorn stacked haybales lining the sidewalk; spider webs cling to various doorways of shops; ghostly kites dance in the wind. Vendors are out with their wares – the mixing scents creating the perfect blend of fall. Children race through the crowd, narrowly avoiding collisions, to wait in line for the carnival-esque rides throughout the area.

As soon as she locks the door, Ellie stands outside of her shop, basking in the surroundings. "Stay still long enough and I might just think you're a part of the decorations."

Ellie laughs at the cheesy line. "Detective John, what a wonderful surprise. How's being the big boss at the precinct?"

Detective John shrugs. "It has its moments. I definitely miss your old man – I didn't have as many worries then as I do now. Shop keeping you busy?"

"As busy as being a florist during the holidays can be," Ellie giggles. "So, what are you supposed to be?"

She looks at the detective who is dressed as normal as one can be on Halloween. "I figured I'd take the day off from wearing anything crazy so I'm your regular Joe-schmoe."

"Sure thing, John."

"I like your swamp-witch vibe you got going on," Detective John attempts a compliment.

"Thanks. I wasn't sure what to be this year, and took inspiration from my buddy Buster," Ellie pets Buster affectionately as he sits on her shoulder.

"I had no idea he was even there," Detective John states. "Can I pet him?"

"Sure, just be careful – he is more delicate than he looks."

Detective John runs a single finger on top of Buster's head, the bearded dragon closing his eyes in contentment. "What's in the bag?"

"Oh," Ellie looks at the large garment bag she is carrying like a baby. "This is Aggie's costume for the contest. I actually made two this year – I'm pretty surprised I was able to do that and keep up with my normal orders."

"Wow." Detective John's eyes widen in surprise. "That is quite the feat. I hope at least one of your costumes does well."

"Thanks, John. I appreciate it."

"Well, I can't stay and chat for too long. I have to go meet up with the mayor before the costume contest begins."

Ellie waves as Detective John walks toward the small city hall. "Catch you later, Joe-schmoe!"

Ellie's phone vibrates in her hand, 'Best Friend <3' taking up the screen with a picture icon. "Just the person I was waiting on. Where are you?"

"You're going to hate me. I'm running late," Aggie whines. "I can't find my shoes for the costume contest – I think I might have left them in the city! I knew this would happen to me."

"We can figure out your shoes. You're wearing a dress made from sunflowers so wear something that matches."

Ellie can feel the eyeroll from Aggie from the other side, "I know you didn't just say that to me. This is your best work, and I must have the best accessories to match! Do you have anything that would work?"

It's Ellie's turn to roll her eyes. "It's a ballgown, Aggie. Nobody will even see your shoes. But yeah, I think I have something in mind for you. Where are you now?"

"At Mom and Dad's place but not to worry – if you have shoes, I will leave now and meet you at the dressing rooms in fifteen minutes. Capiche?"

"Capiche. See you then." Ellie quickly ends the call and heads back into her shop. She fiddles with her keys and unlocks a well-hidden door that leads to the apartment loft upstairs. Ellie fumbles through her collection of shoes before finding some that could match Aggie's costume. She takes a look at the time display on her phone and decides to get to the dressing rooms earlier.

Ellie makes it to the taped off area of dressing rooms for the contestants. Each tent is labelled with their name and entry number. Since she has time to spare, Ellie decides to search for Ivy's tent. It takes her a few minutes, but she stumbles into the tent after tripping on her own high-heeled boot. She double-checks that the garment bag is secure in her hands. "Sorry, Ivy. Didn't mean to pop in unannounced, but I tripped." Ellie announces to an empty tent.

Shrugging her shoulders, Ellie leaves to find Aggie's tent, which happens to be right next door. "Oh, the rivalry continues even outside the city," Ellie sighs.

She pulls back the flaps and enters a modestly decorated tent. There is a small vanity with a lighted mirror, a coatrack for hanging clothing and accessories, and a small table with a chair for guests. Ellie takes a seat in the chair and places Buster on the tabletop. The bearded dragon stomps his feet a few times, nails lightly clicking on the surface, before flopping down dramatically. Ellie shakes her head at his antics. "Sometimes I think you're more dog than lizard, Buster." She affectionately strokes under his chin.

"I'm here, I'm here!" Aggies crashes through the tent. "Can you believe they put me next to Ivy? I swear, it's like the whole town wants us to be at each other's throats." She pauses a moment to catch her breath with her hands on her thighs. "I need to run more. That was insane. You'd think I'm out of shape over here!"

Ellie laughs, "It's not that serious, Aggie. I'm sure it's just an odd coincidence."

Aggie sighs exaggeratedly. "You're probably right. I just want to win! Ivy's won the past three years; I'm just ready to beat her this year. No hard feelings."

"I know. You guys have always had a competitive spirit. So, you ready to get dressed?"

Aggie beams at Ellie. "Of course! Let's get to it."

Aggie strips down to her brown leotard – a must-have for the dancer. Ellie assists in removing the ballgown from the garment bag. Aggie gasps as she sees the dress revealed before her eyes. "If this isn't the most amazing dress I've ever seen!" Aggie squeals. "And I get to wear it!" She pumps her fist in triumph.

"You're such a dork," Ellie grins.

The dress is a ballgown fit for a queen – the Queen of Autumn more precisely. Using that as inspiration, Ellie befitted the large tulle ensemble with sunflowers, orange dahlias, chrysanthemums, and roses. The mesh sleeves are adorned with cascading petals, creating an ethereal effect. "Wow," Aggie whispers reverently.

Ellie beams. "Stunned you to silence? That's a first!"

Aggie playfully glares at her best friend. "Shut up, Ellie! This...this is a masterpiece!"

Ellie bows in appreciation. "Why thank you, my queen. Your humble servant is very honored to have pleased you."

Aggie rolls her eyes. "Now who's the dork? Let's get me in it. The anticipation is killing me."

"You got it." Ellie has Aggie carefully step into the dress, mindful of the florals. The neckline of the dress accentuates Aggie's collar-bones and gives the regal vibe she was looking for.

"Perfect," Ellie states. "Now for your Queen of Autumn crown!"

Aggie bends down a bit for Ellie to add her headpiece – a simple headband with matching flowers and a few crystals to add sparkle. Aggie looks at herself in the mirror and smiles softly. "No matter if I win or lose, this makes me feel so pretty. Thanks again, Ellie."

Ellie holds her by the shoulders, careful not to mess up anything, and smiles at her in the mirror, "No problem at all, Aggie. I hate to run, but I do have to help Ivy with her headpiece as well. I'll be back soon!"

"Sure thing. I'm just going to put the final touches on my make-up, and I'll be good to go. Wait – did you bring me shoes?"

Ellie chuckles and points to the table, "Right over there. Buster, keep an eye on things here. I'll be back!" She waves as she leaves to go to the tent next door.

Ellie clears her throat before speaking above her normal level. "Ivy? It's Ellie. Are you decent?"

"Yes! Come on in, Ellie!" Ivy's voice filters through.

Ellie steps into the tent and sees that Ivy is indeed dressed in her costume. "Wow, you look great, Ivy! I love the addition of the elf ears – very whimsical. I have your headpiece," Ellie reaches into her satchel, "right here."

The circlet features Salal Lemon leaves and blue marvel salvia – a tie-in to the lavender-look-alike appeal of the dress. Ivy squeals her excitement, "It's perfect! Will you be able to put it on with my hair like this?"

Ivy's blonde hair is in a half-up half-down do, some curls pinned atop the crown of her head as the rest cascades down her back. Ellie looks over the style and nods approvingly, "It shouldn't be an issue at all. You have your bobby pins, right?"

Ivy points to a box on the provided vanity. "A dancer never leaves home without them. You never know when you might need one."

"Aggie is the same way," Ellie laughs.

Ivy's eyes shine with friendly competitive light, "How is Aggie? I heard she entered this year and that she has a design by you too."

Ellie finishes pinning the circlet to Ivy's hair and motions with a key-to-lock gesture, saying, "My lips are sealed."

Ivy groans, "A little hint wouldn't hurt?"

At this, the tent flaps open and both women turn to the intruder. "Honey!" Ivy exclaims.

Drew stands starstruck upon viewing Ivy in her costume. "I really am lucky," he sighs dreamily.

The women laugh at his words. "It looks like I'm all done here, Ivy. And the florals all seem to be in good shape. I'll leave you two lovebirds be."

Drew snaps his head to Ellie. "Sorry, Ellie. She's just so lovely. I can't help it." He grins sheepishly.

"Don't be sorry – it's cute. Gives me hope that a swamp-witch like me can find true love." The trio laugh in good spirits, Ellie doing a two-finger salute as she exits Ivy's tent.

—◆O◆—

Ellie languidly walks around the town center, a small container of cinnamon apples in her hand. She munches on the treats as she peers through the vendors' carts of wares. Halloween décor, themed foods, and handmade knick-knacks flash before her eyes. The entire town is in lively spirits – the atmosphere tinged with Halloween anticipation. The weather is perfect for the parade: warm with a slow breeze kicking in every once in a while. Ellie can't help but smile as kids vie for a chance at various carnival games – bobbing for apples, darts, dunk tank, and more. A small boy tries his luck at the high striker; his arms quake as he lifts the foam hammer high above his head before smashing it down onto the platform. The bell does not strike as evidenced by the 'awws' echoing through the crowd. The game operator pats his head as he makes room for the next contestant. Various townspeople wave at Ellie as she passes, a few kids enamored by Buster accompanying her. The dragon relishes the small batches of attention.

A high-pitched squeak rings through loudspeakers. Several people cringe inwards at the intrusive sound. "Apologies for that," a masculine voice clears his throat. "The Whispering Pines Halloween Costume Contest is about to begin. Please make way towards the stage in front of town hall if you wish to attend."

Excited chatter floats through the air as a crowd makes way to the annual costume contest. A makeshift stage sits in front of the town hall. The mayor, an aging man in his last term of office, smiles broadly at the crowd. To his right sits a table of three judges. Ellie spots Mrs. Palmer at the center-seat and waves in acknowledgement. "Welcome everyone," the mayor's voice greets loudly and clearly across the speakers. "To Whispering Pines's Annual Halloween Costume Contest. We are very excited about this year's turn-out. I believe this year will be the best one yet!"

Ellie cheers along with the crowd, caught in the excitement and anticipation of the atmosphere. "Let us begin with the first group of contestants."

A family of five walks across the stage dressed as skeletons. The crowd claps as the judges murmur among each other. The cycle continues as various groups and single costumes grace the stage. "And now, we have the Queen of Autumn!"

Ellie whistles loudly and cheers, "Aggie!"

Oohs and ahs filter through the crowd's applause. Aggie soaks in the positive attention and beams as she shows off Ellie's creation. Mrs. Palmer sends Ellie a big thumbs-up and a wink, clearly showing her approval. Aggie leaves the stage after a few moments and the mayor takes control once again. "Our next contestant is the Woodland Faerie!"

The crowd cheers, but no one enters the stage. Confused whispers mix among the slow clapping of the audience. The mayor looks to the judges, but none give an answer. He hastily waddles to the center of the stage. "It appears as though there may be some confusion. Let us welcome our next group!"

Ellie glances toward the stage in concern but sees no sign of Ivy. "Excuse me," she states as she moves out of the crowd and heads back to the tents housing the costume contest participants. Aggie sees Ellie coming. "That was so fun!" She throws her arms around her best friend.

"You looked amazing out there, Aggie. Like true royalty!" Ellie jokes.

Aggie giggles as she lets go of the hug. "Of course I am. You should refer to me as such from now on."

"How did Ivy look? I wasn't able to see her."

"That's why I came back," Ellie muses. "She never showed on stage."

Aggie raises a brow in question. "That isn't like her. Maybe we should go see what's up?"

"Yeah, I agree. I'm not getting a good feeling about this." Ellie frowns.

Aggie links arms with Ellie. "Let's check on her." She nods resolutely.

The best friend duo walks to Ivy's tent. "Ivy? Drew?" Ellie calls out through the tent flaps.

Drew rushes through the flaps of the tent, "Call 9-1-1! Please!" The desperation in his voice is palpable.

Ellie scrambles for her phone in her satchel. "What happened, Drew?"

The trio enter the tent. Ivy's body lies in a heap on the floor of the tent. Aggie gasps and rushes to her friendly rival. She places her head on her chest, listening for any sign of life. "I don't think she's breathing," Aggie gasps out. "I'm starting CPR. Ellie, tell the operator we're starting compressions. I'll keep going until they get here."

Ellie nods her acknowledgement. "Drew. What happened?" Her stern voice snaps Drew's focus to her instead of Ivy.

"I-I don't know! I went out for a snack and when I came back, Ivy was just lying on the ground. Her breathing was so shallow, and she started getting hives, so I injected her with the Epi-Pen we always carry. She's not responding anymore!" Drew becomes more and more hysterical as Ellie relays the information to the operator on the phone. His eyes are wide and panicked as they observe Aggie giving Ivy CPR.

Within a few minutes, medics arrive to assess Ivy's condition. "She's not responding?" the paramedic asks as CPR is taken over.

"No," Aggie solemnly shakes her head. "I started once we found Drew after Ivy didn't show on stage. Maybe ten-ish minutes."

At that moment, Lily joins the crowd in the tent. "What's going on? Ivy?" She drops her drink in shock, taking in the scene before her.

Drew, Ellie, and Aggie turn to Lily. "There's been an incident, Lily. Ivy had an allergic reaction. We had to call 9-1-1."

Lily's eyes well with worried tears. "She's not dead, is she?"

Drew cries silently while gnawing on his nails. "She needs to get up," Drew shouts, "Why won't she get up?"

"Let them do their job. Let's get out of the tent and give them space." Ellie takes charge of the group. Drew tugs at his hair in frustration and worry. Ellie places a hand on his shoulder as an act of comfort.

A shaky sob escapes Drew's lips, and he throws himself into Ellie's arms. "I need her to be okay, Ellie. I can't live without her." The sentence is barely above a whisper, deep sadness coating his words.

"We will figure it out, Drew." The group stands there as more chaos erupts inside of the tent.

"Move out of the way!" The paramedics exit the tent with Ivy atop a stretcher. Someone is still administering CPR, though Ivy is unresponsive.

"Drew! Go with her." Ellie pushes him to follow the group.

Detective John jogs up to the three women as they watch the ambulance pull away. "I've been called in as a precautionary measure. Nobody is in trouble here. What's going on?"

Ellie sighs and recounts the events leading up to Drew leaving in the ambulance with Ivy. Detective John writes down all the details Ellie provides, but he pins her with a look. "And you didn't use any lavender in her dress?"

"Of course not. She was allergic – highly allergic. I used a substitute: blue marvel salvia. Very similar in look and feel, but definitely not lavender itself. I can get you my records if you need it."

Detective John holds up a finger as his phone rings. "John...yes...yes...damn it." He heaves a deep sigh. "I'll inform her. Thank you."

He clicks to end the call before he turns to Lily. "Lily, can I speak with you privately?"

Lily shakes her head violently. "No, no, no. Don't you dare!"

"I'm so sorry, Lily, but Ivy has passed away from her reaction. I'm going to take you to the hospital so you can be with Drew and inform your family."

Tears stream down the twin's face as a sob escapes her. "Okay."

Detective John shoots Ellie and Aggie a sympathetic glance as he guides Lily away from the tents. Tears prick their eyes. "Tell me this isn't happening, Ellie," Aggie whispers.

Ellie grabs her hand. "I don't want to believe it either."

Ellie is slowly moving on autopilot in her shop when her phone rings with a video call. The contact 'Dad' flashes on the screen. "Hey, Dad."

"Hey, Petunia. I'm calling because I heard about the parade. How are you doing?" Her father's concern brings a small sad smile to her face.

"Well, not exactly alright at the present, but probably better than what Drew and Lily are going through. I can't believe that Ivy's gone. It's all so surreal."

Ellie's dad nods, unease marring his features, "There's more to my call. I've been informed that they're going to be investigating Ivy's death. There are too many questions, and the circumstances are odd. You're going to be interrogated as you made the dress."

Ellie frowns, "I mean, I understand, but I have no reason to harm Ivy."

"I know, hun, but this is the nature of the job. Ivy comes from a powerful family, and they are out for blood. Just cooperate and keep your head down in the meantime."

Ellie raises a skeptical brow. "You're making it sound like I'm a suspect, Dad."

The bell chimes as her shop's door is pushed open. Detective John enters the small space, a troubled expression on his face. "I've gotta go, Dad. Detective John is here. I'll give you a call back later." Ellie presses to end the video chat without hearing a response.

Ellie frowns at the detective. "I'm assuming you're here for my records."

"Among other things. Do you have a few minutes to talk and answer some questions?"

"Sure," Ellie moves to the computer and begins to click through her purchase records. "I'm just printing out everything I invoiced for Ivy's costume. Let's get on with it."

"Ellie, I'm not here to be a bad guy. I'm just trying to do my job. Do you mind if I record?" Detective John shakes a small tape recorder.

Ellie gestures with her hand to consent to the recording. He asks her the basic questions of name, where she was, how she knew Ivy, and more. "And how is Ivy's relationship with Drew?"

"Drew? Oh my god. The two of them could make anyone puke with how sweet they were with each other. I mean that figuratively. Drew and Ivy are hopelessly smitten with each other. No way Drew would be involved in this at all." Ellie vehemently comes to Drew's defense.

Detective John nods along, "And Aggie? Anything interesting there?"

"Aggie! What? John, you can't be serious?" Ellie's incredulous look is no surprise to Detective John.

"We have to cover all of our bases. So, again, Aggie and Ivy's relationship?"

Ellie shakes her head. "They were friendly rivals. But I'm serious when I say that Aggie would never harm Ivy. Hell, she even gave her CPR!"

"I know, Ellie. I'm just doing my job." Detective John continues his questioning, and all the while Ellie becomes more and more agitated at the slight accusations to her friends.

"I think that's everything. I'm sorry again, Ellie." He clicks off the tape recorder.

"I know. This is just so hard to believe." Ellie hangs her head and slumps in defeat.

Detective John eyes her carefully. "Your brain is cooking up something, isn't it?"

"What?" Ellie asks, "No. I have nothing in my mind besides what I told you."

"I know you, Ellie. You're not going to let this go. I'll keep you updated on any news." He takes the records from the countertop, "We'll get to the bottom of this." With that statement, the detective leaves her shop.

Ellie taps her fingers on the glass countertop of her register area, thoughts heavy in her mind. She dials up another video call to her dad. "Hey, Dad. Can I ask you for a favor?"

Ellie's dad grins. "The apprentice has come to play, huh? Need me to make a call?"

⚬

"You know, I'm really not supposed to be doing this," sighs Detective John. "But the Chief called in a favor to the department. Said the two of you used to 'solve all the crimes.'"

"He's just reminiscing, but another pair of eyes never hurts. Can I see the file?" Ellie asks as she shrugs off her coat and places her purse on the floor.

"You could've been a good one, you know?" Detective John looks at Ellie imploringly.

She waves away his comment and smirks. "Then how would you have a job, John?"

Detective John chuckles. "I'm serious. You and your dad are a force when together. Why'd you stop?"

Ellie scrunches her nose in thought. "It never called to me – detective work. Sure, I did the academy and a couple cases with Dad once upon a time, but the passion wasn't there anymore. So, I followed my heart and opened my shop. Dad still tries to lure me back, but I'm happy with my decision."

"You could always consult on the side."

Ellie smirks. "Isn't that what I'm doing right now?"

Detective John hands over the manila folder and shakes his head. "Have at it. We have two suspects – the husband and the rival."

"You're considering Aggie as an actual suspect? Why?"

"They dance at the same company, right? Well, Aggie's competition is gone. She can now have all the roles that they fought over. Pretty convenient timing, too, since they are starting to rehearse for The Nutcracker in December."

Ellie mulls over the information, looking at the case from a law enforcement point of view versus a friend. "Okay, that is a fair point, but Aggie hasn't been in town long enough to sabotage the dress or see Ivy. She didn't even know what flowers were being used nor the fact that Ivy had a severe allergy to lavender. It's not common knowledge."

Detective John hums, "You may be right on that. It still doesn't change the suspicion. And she doesn't have a solid alibi – the Halloween Parade was chaos – and nobody can say for sure where she was before the stage."

"Fine, shaky alibi and motive for Aggie. What about Drew?" Ellie flips through the files and spots some big information. "Woah."

"So, you've found it, huh? Yep – Drew took out a very sizeable life insurance policy on Ivy. Money is always a motive." Detective John crosses his arms and leans back in the rolling chair, the flexible back support squeaking from the force. "It makes a lot of sense – he did know about her allergy and with the life insurance payout he wouldn't need to work another day in his life."

Ellie taps a finger to her chin, "I did see them sign papers the other day when I was checking Ivy's costume during her fitting. Could this be what I saw?"

"It's a possibility. They dated the papers on October 30th, and the policy went into effect immediately. Their lawyers are very good at ensuring their assets are well protected."

Ellie reads through the policy details as Detective John explains. "Hold on a second." She glances at the smug detective. "There is a clause in here – 'In the event of insured's death involving nefarious circumstances, no payout shall be granted to Mr. Drew Ellis as primary beneficiary. All holdings shall therefore be forfeited and issued upon Ms. Lily Blake until proof of innocence is guaranteed and true.'"

Detective John snatches the folder from Ellie's hands. "You've got to be kidding me. There's no way!" His eyes frantically read over the paragraph outlining specific death details and what should happen in each scenario. He groans, "Well there goes that motive. He wouldn't be able to get any payout according to this. But it still sits unwell with me. The whole thing does, honestly."

"I get it," Ellie nods in solemn agreement. "While Ivy and I were never best friends, we were friendly. She was a sweet person."

Ellie combs through the photos of the crime scene. Petals and flowers litter the floor of the small tented space from both Aggie and Ivy's dresses. It takes her several minutes to spot something out of place – a bouquet of flowers standing pretty on the vanity. "These were not in Ivy's tent earlier in the day."

Detective John looks to where Ellie is pointing. "How do you know?"

"Before finding Ivy, I was helping her get ready. I put her circlet on her head – the crown she had on. That vase was not there." Ellie takes the photo and holds it closer to her face, "And from the looks of it, there is lavender in the bouquet. Blue marvel salvia is a bit darker in color and that right there looks like the exact shade Ivy had in mind, but couldn't get. It's hard to tell with an untrained eye, but I'm pretty confident someone close to her gave her that bouquet."

"Okay, so Drew then? He was with her a majority of the day, according to him, and only stepped away to get something to eat." Detective John looks confused as he studies the vase of flowers. "You can really tell what those are based on this photo?"

"It is my job," Ellie laughs in good humor. "But yeah – that is definitely lavender."

"There is one other detail I forgot to mention." Detective John looks over at Ellie, "The autopsy showed minor swelling in Ivy's esophagus."

"Her esophagus? But she died from anaphylaxis. How is that...wait a minute. That means that she could've ingested lavender too. There are teas out there that use lavender as a flavoring agent – you can even make your own tea by steeping the petals."

"Bingo, baby detective. The most severe reaction was skin and airborne based – the amount of pollen in her nasal cavity and on her face confirmed it. But it doesn't account for the esophagus irritation."

Ellie shoots up from her chair, "I think I have an idea of who did it. And it isn't one of your main suspects at all!" She races to grab her things and runs to the door shouting, "Thanks for the look-see at the files! I'll be back with concrete proof!"

"Ellie! Come back!" Detective John calls for her as the door slams shut.

⬤

Ellie waits on the front porch of Ivy and Drew's estate, nervously running her hands through her hair. "Keep it cool, Ellie. Keep it cool. You got this."

The wooden door creaks open to reveal a bloodshot-eyed Drew. "Ellie? What are you doing here?"

"Hey, Drew. I was expecting Rosita to answer the door like usual."

"I gave her some time off to grieve. She's known Ivy all her life. Figured she needed some time to process losing her."

Ellie shows him a small smile. "That's really sweet of you, Drew. Are you taking care of yourself?"

Drew eyes Ellie suspiciously, "I'm...fine. Why are you here?"

"Do you happen to have a minute?" Ellie rushes to hide her nerves with a smile.

"I guess. Come in." He opens the door to let Ellie inside.

"I'm sorry for dropping in unannounced. I know it's been a very hectic few days – I would have come by sooner, but I figured you needed your space."

Drew stares at Ellie blankly. "Has it been days? It feels...time doesn't feel the same anymore."

Ellie places a comforting hand on Drew's shoulder. "I'm so sorry, Drew. Please let me know if there is anything you need."

"Hey!" Lily waltzes into the entryway and stands with her hands on her hips, affronted by Ellie's presence.

Ellie glances at Drew, but he seems to be elsewhere than the present day. "Lily, how are you doing?"

Lily rolls her eyes. "Just peachy. Why are you here?"

"Actually, I came to talk to you. I was hoping you could help me with the floral arrangements for the funeral?" Ellie asks, praying to anyone above that her plan works.

Lily looks her up and down. "Fine," she huffs in annoyance. "This shouldn't take too long anyways."

She turns and Ellie takes that as her cue to follow. Instead of the tea room she visited a few days ago, Lily takes Ellie into the chef's paradise kitchen. "Want a drink?" Lily asks, "It's the host in me that needs to ask."

"Sure, I'll have a drink. What do you have?"

"Water, juice, soda, alcoholic beverages if you want one," Lily lists off.

"What about tea? I've been feeling a bit itchy in my throat and Ivy had mentioned your tea was helping her when she had a cough."

Lily's eyes widen ever-so-slightly, but Ellie catches the facial expression immediately. "Is that okay?" Ellie feigns innocence in her question.

"It was a special recipe for Ivy. I don't think I have all of the ingredients to make it."

"Aw, that's so nice. You guys must've had a strong bond as siblings if you made her a special tea."

"Yeah, we were best friends. Been with each other since day one." Lily stands unmoving at the kitchen island.

"I'm an only child so I can only imagine what having any sibling feels like. Was it fun? Your childhood?" Ellie diverts the topic, secretly hoping to unlock Lily's safe.

A small smile graces Lily's face, so much like Ivy's that Ellie is taken aback. "We had a great time growing up as kids. But the adult life is different."

Ellie clears her throat exaggeratedly, "Wow, I'm parched. Can I take that tea with the ingredients you have? Is that okay?" Ellie questions again.

Lily nods absentmindedly, her body moving around the kitchen on autopilot, "Sure...yeah...yes, of course. One Ivy's Tea coming right up. Anyways, what did you need me for again?"

"The funeral arrangement florals. Drew is very much upset, and as Ivy's twin sister and best friend, I figured you might have a better feeling for what she would have liked." Ellie leans her elbows on the kitchen island.

Lily busies herself with wiping down the clean countertops with a dish towel as the water boils in a tea kettle on the gas-powered stove. "I do know her best, don't I? Hmmm, well she was always a fan of dahlias and hydrangeas for whatever reason. Those should work. And pastel colors I presume – similar to what she had at her wedding. You should be able to figure it out from there."

The tea kettle wails its high-pitched song. Ellie watches as Lily prepares her tea. "Here you are." Lily slides the cup and saucer to Ellie, "One cup of Ivy's Tea."

Ellie takes a sip and is pleasantly surprised by the rich flavors and natural sweetness. "It's good." She swallows, "But it's missing something."

Lily tilts her head. "What is it missing?"

Ellie looks Lily dead in her eyes. "Lavender."

Lily shakes her head. "No. There is no lavender in the tea."

Ellie keeps making eye contact with Lily. "I think you know exactly what I'm getting at, Lily. You're playing dumb right now, but I can see it clear as day. I didn't catch it a few days ago, but I swore I smelt it. Lavender – right when Drew and I walked past you when you gave Ivy tea."

Lily laughs nervously. "There is no way that you smelled lavender because there is no lavender in the tea."

"Prove it," Ellie dares.

"What?"

"Prove it. Let me see your spices and tea leaves." Ellie crosses her arms over her chest.

Lily stands as frozen as ice, a deer caught in headlights. "You're nuts, Ellie."

Ellie tilts her head in question. "So I can't look at your spices and tea leaves?"

"You're not the police. You're a guest. No, you cannot look in my kitchen. What are you even getting at?"

"First off, this isn't even your kitchen. Last I checked, this is Drew and Ivy's home. Ivy even mentioned that you're only a guest the other day. If I ask Drew, do you think he'd let me look around?"

Lily scoffs at Ellie's assumption. "That's pretty bold of you to assume, Ellie. I'm family to Drew. You're just a nobody hired to do a job for us. You should butt out of family business."

Ellie props her elbows on the island and places her chin atop her hands. "There's another reason I'm here."

Lily cocks a brow. "And that would be?"

"I think you killed Ivy."

"Why would I do that? She's my twin sister!" Lily exclaims, arms outstretched wide. "I would never hurt her!"

"Right," Ellie agrees instantly. "I would hope for the same, but things don't add up."

Lily cackles, "That's a bold claim, Ellie. What evidence do you even have to support that?"

Ellie narrows her eyes. "Call it a hunch."

A split-second later Lily runs out of the kitchen. "Drew! You need to help me!" She screeches as she races through the mansion.

Ellie chases after her. "Admit it, Lily! You did it! You killed Ivy!"

"I didn't!" she wails unconvincingly.

Drew comes out from another portion of the house. "What is with all the – oof."

Lily crashes into Drew and sends them spiraling to the floor. "Help me, Drew! She's saying crazy things!" Lily buries her head into Drew's neck to hide from Ellie's stare.

Drew, dazed and confused, simply mutters, "Huh?"

"I think you need to hear this, Drew," Ellie starts, "Lily is the one who killed Ivy."

Drew glances at the woman dramatically wailing into his neck. The seconds that pass by seem to draw out slowly like molasses. "Is that true?" he hoarsely whispers.

Lily stops her caterwauling. "What?"

"Is it true? Did you kill Ivy?" he retorts.

Lily goes limp in his arms before sitting up slowly. "Why would I?" She pouts, waterworks starting to form.

"That's what I don't get either." Ellie places a finger to her chin in false thought. "You were extremely worried at the parade a few days ago. Even cried. You were really convincing."

"I didn't do it, ever think that's why I cried? I'm completely innocent."

"You would've gotten away with it, too, if it weren't for the bouquet." Ellie hits.

"What bouquet?" Drew asks, "There was no bouquet, right?"

"I saw the photos of the scene, Drew. And on top of Ivy's vanity was a vase of flowers. Some of them were lavender."

"What?" Drew whispers in shock. "But there couldn't be. She's allergic."

"Exactly. And who knew of that allergy besides me and you?" Ellie lets her question linger in the air.

Drew looks at Lily who is still on top of him in a crumpled pile of limbs. "What did you do?"

Lily gazes into Drew's eyes, the locks coming undone on her safe. "I did it. She had it all – the talent, the personality, the life. And most of all, she had you! I loved you first. It was me. It should have been me!"

Lily hits Drew in the chest. "You were supposed to be mine! And now you can be mine!"

Hysterical, Lily grabs Drew's face. "Now we can be in love without her in the way! Just as it was always meant to be. Remember the old days, Drew?"

Drew's eyes, wide with fear, cast a quick glance to Ellie, who remains silent. He slowly shakes his head, not recalling a single instance where he gave Lily the same attention he gave Ivy. "We used to go out all the time, just the two of us. But then she came along and ruined everything. I'm glad she's dead! I'm glad she's gone!"

Lily takes Drew's silence as permission and kisses him. He doesn't fight her off, too shocked and overwhelmed to do anything but process the information. "That should do it," Ellie takes her phone out of her satchel. "Did you get all that, Detective John?"

"Yep. Thank you, Ellie. Okay men, let's get in there." The phone call ends with a click, but the screen recording keeps going.

Drew pushes Lily off and wipes his mouth with the back of his hand. He gags slightly at kissing another woman as he stands up. "How could you?" he yells imploringly. "She was nothing but nice to you!"

Lily looks astonished that Drew pushed her off, carefully touching her lips as she kneels on the ground. "But you love me...we were meant to be together, Drew."

"You're insane." Drew backs away and shakes his head. He draws in on himself once more as officers enter the house and find the trio.

"Lily, you're going to need to come with us," Detective John states evenly, spooking the murderer as clarity comes to her.

"No, I was only kidding," she pleads as another officer places her into handcuffs and reads her Miranda Rights. "It wasn't me. I'd never do it. Drew!" Her shrill voice echoes through the mansion, "Drew! Help me. Drew, I love you!"

Ellie and Drew watch as she is dragged from the house. Ellie turns to the heartbroken man. "How did I not see it?" he hoarsely whispers, tears threatening to spill.

"It wasn't all too obvious, Drew. Nobody could have predicted this."

"What am I going to do now?" His eyes appear frightened at the possibility of being alone.

"We will help you get through it," Ellie promises and opens her arms for an embrace, allowing Drew to come to her.

Drew takes the small comfort. "Thank you, Ellie."

Drew walks her to the front door after they're questioned once more by the police. "Drew," Ellie pauses. "Please let me know if you need help with anything. You're still a friend to me, no matter what has happened."

A sad smile stains Drew's lips. "I know. You're a good friend, Ellie. Thank you for finding Ivy justice. I'll see you at the funeral."

The case of the Whispering Pines Halloween Costume Contest Murder closes with the door of Drew and Ivy's home.

Kristen Elizabeth

Thank you for reading Love, Lies, and Lavender! I had such a blast writing Ellie and crew in her 'debut' as a neighborhood sleuth. To keep up with me online, please follow me on social media via Instagram: authorkristenelizabeth. Happy reading!

Chapter Four

Mystery of the Missing Heirloom

Juliet E. Sidonie

Thursday, October 29, 1942

Deloris had just opened the door and was ready to head out for a night on the town with her girlfriends when the phone rang. She ran back inside and answered in her best posh, professional voice, "Miss Markham Investigations, Kansas City's superlative detective service. To whom am I speaking?"

There was a giggle, and then an even more hoity-toity voice answered back, "It is I, Mrs. Alphia Lansdale, of Jameson, Missouri. Surely, you've heard of me. I should very much like to speak to Miss Deloris Markham if she could possibly be available."

Deloris burst out laughing, as did her caller. "I have heard of you. Alfie, how are you?" Deloris asked her dear friend, whom she'd known since high school. "I wasn't expecting you to call."

Alfie snickered. "I'm okay, DeDe, but I do need your help investigating something. Is there any way you could come up for a visit this weekend?"

"I should be able to," Deloris replied, "but what do you need investigated?"

"I'll tell you when you get here," Alfie said, "because I know you'll show up if I don't tell you. You can't resist an unsolved mystery. Plus, then we can celebrate Halloween together."

Deloris laughed and replied, "Miss Markham Investigations, at your service, not only in Kansas City but also in the wilds of northern Missouri."

Friday, October 30, 1942

After several hours on the highway in a crowded bus, Deloris arrived at the Pattonsburg bus station just as the sun was setting. It was a warm October, and the stars were twinkling in the dusk. Alfie was there waiting, and the two young ladies loaded Deloris's suitcase into the sedan and headed east to Jameson, their hometown.

The road that Alfie drove to Jameson followed the railroad tracks. It was the shortest route between the two towns, but Deloris never liked going that way because the road was rough and lonely. In the moonlight, tree limbs cast a wicked silhouette against the sky, looking like skeletal hands reaching out to grab whoever dared cross their paths.

As they rounded a bend, Alfie had to brake sharply as they came across a tractor pulling a wagonload of teenagers on a hayride through the dark country roads. The kerosene lanterns that hung from the wagon cast eerie shadows, and a boy at the front of the wagon looked like he was telling a ghost story.

"I'm going to hang back so that my car headlights don't ruin the atmosphere," Alfie said.

"Okay—what's that?" Deloris asked. The young ladies watched as two scarecrows in the cornfield at the side of the road came to life and started chasing the wagon. Peals of laughter mixed with screams erupted from the teenagers. The girls moved closer to the boys, and the boys, with big grins on their faces, put their arms around the girls to protect them from the scarecrows. Then the scarecrows hopped aboard the wagon and took off their masks, revealing two more teenagers.

Alfie and Deloris laughed and started reminiscing about their own memories of past hayrides in the country. The two married women finished each other's stories as they followed the hay wagon.

At the next intersection, the tractor turned right, and the lights from the hayride lanterns quickly faded into darkness. Alfie and Deloris were alone again, with only their headlights to light the way to Jameson. When they got to the covered metal truss bridge over Big Creek, Alfie sped up as quickly as she could across the rickety wooden bridge deck that had several slats missing.

"Slow down!" Deloris protested as she held on to her door and looked at the muddy water below that glistened in the moonlight.

"Sorry, I can't," Alfie replied. "If I go too slow, I'm afraid that one of my tires will get caught in one of the holes where it's missing a slat."

Deloris held her breath as Alfie navigated across the bridge. Alfie only slowed down slightly as she came to the end of the bridge, where the wooden bridge deck was smoother and sturdier and no slats were missing. When they successfully crossed Big Creek and came to the end of the bridge, both ladies let out a sigh of relief, but the relief was short-lived.

Suddenly, a man with a full scraggly beard, dressed in a black overcoat and hat, jumped out in front of their car, blocking them from exiting the bridge. Alfie jammed on the brakes and the startled women screamed. The tires skidded, and the car stopped, barely missing the man who then hit the hood of her car with his fist. He stared at both women menacingly as he continued to block their exit. He then started yelling and flailing his arms.

"What do you think you're doing out here driving that fast? You crazy woman! I have half a mind to..."

The man started walking toward Alfie's door, but as soon as he went to the side of the hood, Alfie put the car in gear and stomped on the accelerator. The man jumped out of the way of the side-view mirror, which almost hit him as the car lurched forward. Alfie's tires spun for a second until they finally took hold, and the car raced away on the dirt road, leaving him in a cloud of dust. They could still hear him yelling obscenities after them a half a mile down the road.

After she caught her breath and her heart stopped racing, Deloris asked, "Who was that?" By then, the angry man was out of sight, engulfed by the cover of darkness.

"Wilbur Whetstone," Alfie answered in almost a squeak. As her voice recovered and she calmed down, she related, "They say he's gone off his rocker since his wife died unexpectedly this spring.

There are whispers he was the one who killed her. She'd come into town with bruises before. He was working in his father's store, but he quit going in and stopped doing everything. Now he wanders around stealing food and whatever else he needs and has been accused several times of attacking people when they catch him. A woman up near Coffey said he tried to assault her in her own home. I just didn't want to find out what would happen tonight. That's why I sped off."

"I'm very glad you did what you did," Deloris said, "but that poor man."

Alfie nodded. "A couple of folks tried to talk to Wilbur, but he didn't listen. He just got mad and shoved them away. Now he basically lives on the streets and what handouts he can get from sympathetic individuals." Alfie shook her head and said, "Enough about him. On a different note, are you planning to go see your parents while you are up here?"

"Oh yes. My mother would never forgive me if I was up here and didn't come for Sunday dinner with all the family. She will expect you there too," Deloris said with a wink.

"How could I turn down Nannie Markham's hot rolls and burnt sugar cake? I hope those are on the menu," Alfie said with a grin.

"I'll put in your request," Deloris laughed.

Deloris and Alfie were silent for the rest of the drive into town, wrapped in their own thoughts about Wilbur. The road was quiet, and only one vehicle, a truck with an advertisement painted on the side, passed them going the opposite direction. When the lights of

Jameson came into view, Deloris realized she still didn't know what Alfie's mystery was about.

"We haven't talked yet about why I'm here, Alfie. What is it you want me to investigate?"

"Did I ever tell you about my grandmother's ring?" Alfie asked. Deloris shook her head no. "It's my inheritance, along with the house. I need you to help me find it."

"An antique ring? Is it valuable? I remember your grandmother. She was a grand lady."

"Probably, but that's not the reason I need to find it," Alfie said as she pulled the car up to her house. "It's late. I'll explain more tomorrow."

"Yes," said Deloris, with a grin on her face. "We'll get some sleep and start the treasure hunt in the morning."

Saturday, October 31, 1942

The next morning, Alfie offered Deloris a cup of coffee and started fixing eggs for breakfast. Deloris looked around the tidy, bright kitchen, and her attention was caught by a stack of letters carefully tucked in an out-of-the-way corner. Deloris had a similar stack from her husband on her nightstand back in Kansas City, so she knew exactly what they were: letters home from the front lines.

"How is your husband doing?" Deloris asked.

"As well as can be," Alfie replied, as she brought two plates, piled high with a jumble of fried eggs, potatoes, and peppers. "How is your husband?"

"He was fine in his last letter, but you never know what the next one will say," Deloris said ruefully. "I read the Marines were involved in a battle with the Japanese on Guadalcanal a few weeks ago. It's driving me crazy not knowing where he is."

"I understand," Alfie nodded.

There was a silence as both young wives were lost in thought. After a minute, Deloris said, "I know it's not the same this year with all the men gone away, but what are the townsfolk doing for Halloween?"

"There aren't any big festivities this year. There's still some trick-or-treating for the little ones, but they're concerned about vandalism, so everyone's supposed to be off the streets early. And with the sugar rationing, candy-making isn't happening. But I've got some cider, and I used some ration coupons to purchase sugar to make popcorn balls yesterday before picking you up. There's a pumpkin to carve, and I thought we could roast the seeds as we listen to the radio tonight after we get back from my grandma's house."

"Why are we going to your grandmother's house?"

Alfie smiled. "Because that's where the ring might be."

"Spill the beans," Deloris said, and Alfie began her explanation as the young women ate their breakfast.

"The ring is a family heirloom. Back in 1852, my four-times great-grandmother married the second son of a British baron. His brother, the firstborn, who would be some kind of great-great-great-uncle to me, inherited the barony, the estate, everything. The only thing the younger son got was a ring, passed down from his mother. She gave it to him, for him to give to his bride on their wedding day. It is a stunning ring, Deloris. It's a two-carat oval blue sapphire surrounded by a circle of twelve small rose-cut diamonds and then a second circle of sixteen smaller sapphires on a gold band."

"Sounds beautiful," Deloris said.

"It is. Hopefully, I'll get to show it to you. Anyway, once my four-times great-grandparents got married, they moved to the United States and had several children. Then, he was killed, fighting for the North in the Civil War. It was hard for his widow, taking care of the family, but she never sold the ring. When she died, the ring passed down to their eldest daughter, my three-times great-grandmother. And it's been passed down to the oldest daughter ever since. Until my grandmother passed away this summer."

"Who inherited the ring when your grandmother died?"

"Well, it was supposed to be my Aunt Theodora. She was older than my mother. But my grandmother disinherited her years ago when she married a Southerner who was also a good-for-nothing thief. Said she would not give the ring to the folks who were responsible for my four-times great-grandfather's death and then have them pawn it off."

"So, it would have gone to your mother? Except she'd already passed, so it would go to you."

"Yes, I've known for years that I'd get the ring. After my mother died from the flu when I was five, my grandmother showed it to me for the first time and told me it would be mine. And that I'd be connected to my mother, my grandmother, and all the other women in my family through the ring. That just like I got my mother's smile, I'd get her ring, and we'd always be connected." Alfie sniffed back a tear.

"Oh, Alfie," Deloris said, as she gave her friend a hug.

"Grandmother didn't like to talk about the ring, and she never wore it, because she didn't want her friends in Jameson to think she was showing off or acting better than them. The only other time I've seen the ring was last summer, just after I got married. When she took it out of the velvet storage bag, a prong caught on the material, and she noticed it needed to be bent back. She had me try it on before I drove her to the jewelers to fix the loose prong and have it cleaned. She showed me the ring because wanted to convince me to have a daughter as soon as possible so that she could be sure the ring would keep on being passed down as a family heirloom. My cousin Eugenia, Aunt Theodora's daughter, already has two girls, so if I didn't have a daughter, Grandmother was afraid the ring would end back up on the other side of the family."

"Did your grandmother keep the ring at her house?"

"I think so. After she showed it to me, I tried to talk her into storing the ring in a safe deposit box at the Jameson Farmers Bank, but she didn't trust banks. She even kept her cash at home. When she died, we found money hidden in a trunk in the attic."

"Did she leave a will?"

"Yes, it was in the trunk, too, along with the deed to the house and the paperwork for a small annuity she had. All the important papers were in the trunk, but the ring wasn't there."

"And she never told you where she kept it?"

"All she told me was that she'd keep it close and hidden safely away until it was time. And then, no one expected her to have a heart attack. We just didn't know it was coming."

"So, no one knows where the ring is?"

"No. I searched the house from top to bottom and didn't find anything."

"Well," Deloris said, "that was before you brought me on the case."

<hr>

After breakfast, the young women went to the house of Alfie's grandmother. As they walked up the long driveway to the big, white two-story residence, Deloris could see that it needed a coat of paint and some tender loving care. Built in 1888, it stood firm against midwestern winters and summer storms, but now the old gal was showing her age. The wrap-around porch broke in the middle for the steps leading up to a big picture window. On each side of the house at the end of the porch was an entry door, making it confusing which door was considered the front door. Gardens that had mostly gone to seed surrounded the house except for a few brave chrysanthemums near the front porch. The grass needed mowing, and the gravel driveway, that curved off to the horse stable in the back of the house, had weeds growing through the rocks. Deloris knew that with most of the men off to war, projects like painting were put on hold, but it made her sad to see the house so neglected and overgrown.

She shook off the sadness, though, because Alfie needed her to focus on finding the ring. They started from the back porch. They moved everything around, turned over pots, and shook out boots. Alfie's grandpa's overcoat still hung on a hook next to her grandmother's coat, just as they did when both grandparents were alive. Alfie searched through the pockets of one coat and Deloris searched the other.

When they entered the house through the back door, Deloris saw the kitchen was still completely furnished. A layer of dust lay over everything, and, through the doorway to the living room, Deloris could see a sofa and two upholstered chairs that were covered by large pieces of fabric. She stopped and looked over at Alfie.

Seeing the question on Deloris's face, Alfie offered, "I haven't gotten rid of anything yet until I find the ring. It surprised me that the house sold last week. I really didn't think that it ever would. It's been on the market for several months. I've got the estate auction scheduled in two weeks, and the new owners will take possession on the first of December. I really need to find the ring so that I can begin the cleanout."

"So, everything is exactly as your grandmother left it when she died?"

"Yes," Alfie replied. They moved to the kitchen and looked it over from top to bottom. Deloris brought a stepstool in from the garden shed, located off to the side of the house, so that they could take a closer look at everything near the ceiling in each room and on top of all the doors, even though Alfie protested her grandmother wouldn't have climbed the stool to hide the ring. "She was shorter than you," Alfie told Deloris, but Deloris just grinned and kept on looking. By noon, they'd gone through each room on the first floor systematically with no luck.

"Let's take a break, go back to my house, and have some lunch. Then we can resume our search afterward," Alfie suggested.

After lunch, they started on the second floor, looking under beds and in wardrobes. They questioned themselves when they shook out the quilts which made them cough at the dust that flew around them. They looked in boxes, pockets, and shoes. Alfie went through her grandmother's undergarments and Deloris looked in her sewing basket. The old wooden box that held a few pieces of costume jewelry didn't yield the ring either. They searched for a hidey-hole everywhere, knocking on walls to see if there was anything hollow, but found nothing. Deloris checked the wooden floorboards and under pieces of furniture. The search of all the rooms on the second floor was fruitless. The day was slipping away, and disappointment was all over Alfie's face.

"We still have tomorrow, and lots to search: the attic, basement, garden shed, and old outhouse out back. It could be in any of them," Deloris said, trying to sound enthusiastic, but Alfie slumped in a chair and started to sniffle. "And I can take another day off from work if need be." Alfie managed a wan smile, and Deloris convinced her to resume the quest tomorrow.

"Tonight," Deloris said, as they locked up and headed back to Alfie's house, "we'll relax and celebrate Halloween."

After cleaning the dust off of their clothes, the two women seated themselves at the kitchen table. Alfie warmed up the cider on the stove while Deloris took a paring knife and started working on her jack-o'-lantern. She cut around the stem and took it out before switching to a spoon to scrape out the seeds. Alfie brought Deloris a pie pan to put the seeds in and followed it up with a cup of steaming hot apple cider. She poured herself a cup of apple cider and took a seat at the kitchen table across from Deloris. She picked up another paring knife and started on her jack-o'-lantern when the phone rang.

The two shared a look of foreboding. During wartime, every time the phone rang or men in uniform showed up at your door, everyone dreaded what the purpose of the call or visit might be, especially if it was in the evening.

Alfie murmured, "Excuse me," and steadied herself at the table before hurrying to the telephone table in the hallway.

Deloris nervously bit her lip and crossed her fingers for luck that the call wasn't from the War Department. She heard Alfie say, "Oh, no!" and then, "Thank you for telling me. We'll be right over." Good, she thought in relief, the call was about something local, not about Alfie's husband.

However, when she came back into the room, Alfie still had a look of worry on her face. Concerned why her friend was still worried, Deloris asked, "What is it?"

"That was Lara O'Casey," Alfie replied. "She saw lights in the windows at my grandmother's house just now. She saw us leave earlier, so she knew it wasn't us. From her kitchen window at her farmhouse, she has a good view of my grandmother's house down the road. She knew no one should be in the house late at night, not after we left. That is why she called here to make sure it wasn't one of us still there."

The phone rang again and when Alfie came back from answering it, she relayed to Deloris that Lara called the Daviess County Sheriff's office.

"She said that the sheriff and his deputy were working a car accident south of Gallatin near the county line. So, it will take a while for them to get here and whoever is in the house might be gone by then."

"It's probably nothing serious, just some kids poking around." Deloris tried to reassure her friend. "It is Halloween, remember? And you have a potential haunted house there."

"Yes," Alfie replied, "I suppose you are right. Just some kids looking to scare themselves, but it could be something more."

"More than hooligans?" Deloris questioned.

"Well, Mrs. O'Casey also said that Wilbur Whetstone was spotted in town today."

"I know he's scary, but there's no reason he should be at your grandmother's house. Or even if he is, he might just be looking for a place to sleep." Deloris tried to reassure her.

Alfie still looked tense, as she opened up the junk drawer and started rifling around until she found a flashlight, which she handed to Deloris. "Will you go back up there with me to check it out and help me search for the ring one last time tonight if we don't find anyone there?"

"Of course," Deloris said.

Alfie knew Deloris had a sense of fearlessness and solving a mystery like who was in the house late at night was right up her alley.

Relieved, Alfie nodded and picked up her solid maple wood rolling pin. Deloris checked to make sure her flashlight worked and nodded in return before saying, "Let's go."

It was already dark as the two friends set out for the house, but Deloris didn't turn on her flashlight. A cantaloupe-colored full moon shone brightly enough to light their way. The streets were quiet, though several windows in the houses they passed were brightly lit; it appeared that most of the Jameson residents were celebrating Halloween indoors. Deloris was glad of the lights and occasional snatches of music trickling out from the houses as they punctuated the night with bits of cheerfulness. Both coasts of the United States had blackout orders to protect cities and ships from view of the enemy, but that part of the war had not reached the cozy little village of Jameson located in the middle of the United States.

Because gasoline was starting to be rationed and Alfie's car was low on the precious fuel, they decided to walk the four blocks out of town past the Jameson City Park. The park, usually busy with children's voices during the day as they played on the teeter-totter, swings, and merry-go-round, was oddly quiet at night. One swing, swaying in an errant breeze, creaked on its chains. It made an eerie, ghostly sound, and the movement looked as if it was luring someone to come sit. The jungle gym cast a strange shadow on the grass.

"Do you feel like someone is watching us?"

"It's a small town, Alfie. Everyone is watching us."

"I still get nervous when I walk by the bandstand, because, you know. His ghost could be out to get us."

Deloris didn't believe the rumors, but she heard there were stories about the park's bandstand being haunted. A body had been found there years ago, that of a man who was mean and not missed. A few months after Deloris graduated from high school in 1931, she solved the fourteen-year-old murder mystery - although the records would never show the truth of the murderer.

"He should be happy that I solved his murder and not haunt us," Deloris said, with a twinkle in her eye at Alfie, who tried to smile back. Deloris was more concerned with the living now, and with whoever turned lights on in the house of Alfie's grandmother.

Alfie still held her breath as they approached the wooden structure of the bandstand. She relaxed a little once they passed the bandstand and were standing at the corner of Kodiak and Fifth Street. They could see the O'Casey farmhouse directly ahead on the left of Kodiak Road and her grandmother's house further beyond it, on the same side of the road.

As they crossed the street and walked toward the O'Casey's house, Alfie and Deloris looked up the road at her grandmother's house. Situated across a big open field from the O'Casey farmhouse, it lay beyond the outskirts of the town and almost to 13 Highway. Even though they gazed at the house, they saw no lights flickering in its windows.

A door creaked open at the O'Casey farmhouse, spilling light out into the crisp fall night, and Lara O'Casey stepped onto her porch. "Are you girls headed up to the house now?"

"Yes," Alfie said. "Thanks for calling me."

"I haven't seen any lights since I called. Maybe whoever it was has gone."

"Fingers crossed," Alfie replied. "But I brought my rolling pin, just in case."

"You call out if you need any help," Lara said, "and let me know what you find out."

"We will," Deloris reassured, "but it was probably just some kids poking around an old, deserted house on Halloween."

Lara nodded and said, "Well, be careful. I just hope it isn't that Wilbur fellow. Everyone in town is talking about him." Deloris and Alfie assured Lara they would be cautious, said their goodbyes, and headed down the road.

"The thing is," Alfie began, breaking the silence. "I get a feeling that it's probably more than a prank or some Halloween trick."

"You think someone else is trying to find your ring?"

"By 'someone' you mean my relatives, right?" Alfie sighed. "Maybe, I don't know. I'd hate to think it was them, but who else could it be?"

"Why would anyone else want to break in? There's furniture, sure, but not really anything worth stealing."

"True. The will, the cash, and all the papers are in the bank now, and I'm sure everyone in Jameson knows that. You know how it is in small towns. It's hard to keep a secret."

"There are three options for who could be in the house this late," Deloris said. "A Halloween hooligan; a vagabond, like Wilbur, looking for a place to stay; or one of your relatives looking for the ring. Who else knows about the ring besides your family and what relatives might search for it?"

"No one but my family knows about the ring. My grandmother never talked about it outside of the family. Let's see, of my relatives, it could be my Aunt Theodora or her daughters, Ossie or Elsea. Her husband died a few years back. Or it could be one of my Uncle Earl's two sons looking for it. Uncle Earl doesn't get around as well anymore, so I doubt he'd be sneaking about at night. His wife passed away several years ago, but the boys always were a little wild. I hate to think that, though, they're all the family I have and the only ones still talking to me. My Aunt Theodora and her girls stopped talking to me when my grandmother died."

When they arrived at the house, everything was quiet and dark, but then Deloris saw something. The shadows were moving on the lawn behind the house. She put a finger to her lips and pointed. Alfie nodded, and Deloris quietly led the way around to the side of the house. Peering around the corner, the women saw a light flickering in a downstairs window. It disappeared and then reappeared a few seconds later.

Alfie and Deloris crept up to the back door, where Alfie handed her rolling pin to Deloris. She took a key out of her pocket and quietly unlocked the back door. She put the key back in her pocket, tightly gripped the rolling pin that Deloris handed back to her, and whispered, "Are you ready?" Deloris nodded. Alfie took a deep breath and opened the door.

———◆O◆———

Leaving the back door open to avoid the sound of it closing, the two women stepped inside and walked on tiptoe to the kitchen. Though only a thin trickle of moonlight came in from the window, Deloris didn't turn the flashlight on. She wanted to surprise whoever it was in the house. Alfie led the way, walking around the kitchen table toward the hallway. Deloris followed but bumped into a chair, which scraped across the floor. The women froze.

For a minute, there was complete stillness in the house. Then, an eerie moaning sound floated down the hallway. Alfie grabbed Deloris's hand as the moaning got louder. When they entered the hallway, something flickered in the darkness. A large opaque, gently floating form came toward them. Suddenly, the form was on top of them, covering them, trapping them.

Alfie and Deloris both screamed when they felt the something engulf them. The screaming made them both cough, as whatever it was covering them was also dusty. Deloris tried to turn her flashlight on while Alfie grabbed for it, which resulted in the flashlight dropping to the ground. Amid the coughing and frantic scrambling to find the flashlight, Deloris managed to pull off whatever it was that had covered them. The metal of the flashlight gleamed in the dim moonlight that was peeking through the big living room window. The moonlight allowed Deloris to find the flashlight, pick it up, and turn it on. Once they had a little light, Alfie, still clutching her rolling pin, found the light switch and turned on the living room lights. The friends stood there blinking like toads in a hailstorm. The large opaque, gently floating form that had covered them turned out to be the old, dusty sheet that had covered the sofa.

"Did you see whoever it was that covered us in the sheet, or where they went?" Deloris asked.

"No, not even a glimpse," Alfie replied regretfully. "Do you think it was my grandmother's ghost or the ghost from the bandstand?"

"Neither. That was a human. I just don't know where they went. Come on, let's investigate." Deloris looked at Alfie, who was still shaking. "Can you turn on all the lights when we enter a room?"

"I can do that." Alfie nodded determinedly.

One room at a time, Alfie turned on the lights and Deloris opened closet doors, looked under beds, and pulled the sheets off of the furniture while Alfie stood ready with her rolling pin to hit whatever or whoever they found lurking under them. When they'd checked the entire house and no one was found, they decided to walk around the outside of the house looking for a source of entry. Deloris shone the flashlight on all the exterior windows and doors until they found a window with a pane of glass broken out, the sill raised halfway up, and a bucket placed under the window.

"Look at this," Deloris said. "I bet this is how the person entered the house. A ghost wouldn't need a bucket or a window."

Alfie smiled and said, "It proves they are human and not a ghost."

"Yes, but whoever it was obviously knows the layout of the house, since this window is hidden from view on the backside of the house where Lara wouldn't see it. Also, they knew they'd need a bucket that they could step up on to get into the window. Plus, they could disappear so quickly."

"Maybe it is the couple buying the house?" Alfie offered. "They've been here several times to view the property."

"No, I don't think so. Why wouldn't they just wait until when they take possession of the house? I'm sorry, Alfie, but it was probably one of your relatives."

Alfie nodded, sighed, and said, "Let's go back inside and block up this window." But just as they turned to go back inside the house, they heard an unexpected noise. Startled, they grabbed each other as an owl hooted and coasted on silent wings closely near them. They only exhaled once the bird was out of sight, and then they started giggling.

Confident they had everything secured on the main level of the house after they put a small board in the bedroom window to block it from opening, Deloris unlocked the door to the basement stairs, but Alfie hesitated.

"Shall we go down to the basement now?" Deloris asked.

"No. I mean, not yet. We still need to search the attic."

"I really think we should go down there now and get it out of the way."

"Really? We have to go down there?"

"Why? What are you afraid of finding down there?"

"I've just always been afraid of the basement and its musty, moldy smell. There are mice and rats down there. Rats as big as a cat! I've seen them. And snakes! I hate snakes."

"We'll hold off going down there until the last thing if you wish, but we need to make sure no one is down there and it is better to do it now. Unless you want to wait until it gets even later at night?"

"Oh, okay," Alfie said. "Might as well get it over with, but you have to go down the stairs first."

Deloris and Alfie started down the dark stairs to the basement. The steps, carved out of the rock that formed the foundation under the house, were narrow and the dirt that covered them made them a little slick. Holding the flashlight in one hand and the wooden handrail in the other, Deloris found the chain to the single lightbulb that hung at the bottom of the steps and pulled it. It lit up briefly and then there was a pop and it went out.

"Great," Alfie almost screamed.

"We've got a flashlight. We'll be fine."

The basement was small, and other than shelves of canned goods and a wringer washing machine, there wasn't any place for a person to hide down there. They quickly checked over the washing machine and the cans but found nothing. As they climbed back up the stairs, a commotion occurred at the basement door just as they arrived at it. Deloris flung the door open in time to see someone dressed in black flee through the back door and run outside. Deloris started to give chase, but Alfie grabbed her arm and said, "Let them go. They could be dangerous, and I don't want you to get hurt. You are more valuable to me than whatever they want."

"Are you sure? I could..."

"I'm sure. Look at it this way—now we know it wasn't a ghost that attacked us earlier. It was definitely a human. And I don't want them hurting you. Come on. Let's go upstairs and see if we can find the ring."

"First, I'm going to find something to protect myself." Deloris went to the kitchen and grabbed a heavy cast iron frying pan. Alfie still held her rolling pin, and Deloris, feeling properly armed with the frying pan, turned toward the stairs when something out of the corner of her eye stopped her. Deloris flashed the light outside and saw the door to the shed was open.

"Where are you going?" Alfie inquired as she came into the kitchen.

"I'm going out to the shed."

"Why? I thought I talked you out of doing that."

"Someone is in there and I want to catch them."

Deloris ran out the back door and entered the shed, with Alfie following several steps behind. When Deloris stepped inside, someone who was inside the shed hiding behind the door rushed up to her back and pushed her.

The person pinned Deloris to the wall and Deloris felt something poke her in the back. The person said, "Stick 'em up, Alfie! I assume you found the ring by now. Give it to me or you die."

"Wrong. I'm not Alfie," Deloris said. "She is."

The person whirled around and in a single movement, Alfie came inside the shed and swung her rolling pin like a baseball bat, knocking out the person who fell to the ground in a heap. "It's a woman," Deloris said, as she looked for the gun, but she didn't find one. It must have fallen away somewhere, but Deloris hadn't heard it fall.

"Turn your flashlight on their face, Alfie, and let's see who this is."

"Elsea!" Alfie gasped. "What are you doing here?"

Coming to, Elsea looked up into her cousin's eyes and groaned, knowing she was caught. Elsea started spewing hateful words at Alfie. "You don't deserve that ring. It should go to my mother. She is the rightful heir."

"You know our grandmother didn't want her to have it, and it was her decision to make," Alfie replied. "She knew that your mother would probably sell it and it is meant to be an heirloom."

"Where is your gun?" Deloris interjected. "You threatened me!"

"Gun?" Elsea sneered. "Oh yeah, I don't have one. I just used my finger to pretend I had a gun. Plus, you two aren't so brave. You were afraid of a sheet!"

"You had me scared half to death!" Alfie exclaimed. Exasperated, she turned to Deloris and said, "Will you call the sheriff again, please? He should be here by now, I would think. The phone by the front door is still connected."

"Okay, but let's take Elsea with us to the house. I don't want to leave you out here with her."

Alfie and Deloris hoisted Elsea onto her feet, while she asked incredulously, "You're going to call the sheriff on me? I'm your cousin."

"For breaking and entering and burglary and death threats? Yes." Alfie said.

Elsea was still shaky from the blow, and she leaned heavily on Alfie as they all walked slowly toward the back door. Once inside, Deloris turned on the light in the kitchen and then turned on the light in the hallway. They made their way down the hallway toward the front door, to where the telephone was located, near the entrance to the living room.

As Deloris picked up the receiver to call the county sheriff, she looked out the window onto the front porch. In shock, she set the receiver back on the hook, forgetting to make the call. "Alfie," Deloris whispered to her friend, "look!" From the dimly lit hallway light shining out of the big glass picture window, Deloris could see there was something large and dark lying on the porch, but Alfie couldn't see anything from her perspective, and she didn't want to let go of Elsea.

"Wait here with Elsea, and I'll check it out."

Alfie nodded, and Deloris gripped her flashlight in one hand and the cast-iron skillet in the other. She slowly opened the front door and gasped when her flashlight revealed a man. There was something unnatural about the way he lay crumpled there. As Deloris got closer, she could see a dark splotch on the back of his jacket and that the man wasn't breathing. She touched the dark splotch and red blood came off on her finger. Then she discovered the body was still slightly warm. Rigor mortis hadn't set in yet, so he hadn't been dead very long. Deloris surmised that the man on the porch must have been killed just before Deloris and Alfie arrived or when they were in the shed. Deloris was numb at the thought that they were that close to someone being murdered and could have been killed too.

Deloris went back to Alfie and Elsea and whispered an explanation. "Right outside the front door on the porch, there's a dead man, and he was just killed…" She looked at Elsea when she said this.

Alfie gasped and whirled around to confront Elsea. "Did you kill him?"

"What, me? No! I don't even own a gun."

"No, he was stabbed, not shot. Do you have a knife?"

"NO!" Elsea replied emphatically and started crying.

From her reaction, Deloris didn't believe Elsea killed him. "If she didn't kill him," Deloris pointed out, "Then whoever did may still be here."

Alfie gasped.

"Might still be here," Elsea repeated, looking pale. "Can we just get out of here?"

"We need to wait for the sheriff," Deloris responded.

"Where is that sheriff? We've got to call him again and say that it is an emergency to get him here sooner," Alfie said.

"I know," said Deloris. "I could run down to the O'Casey farmhouse to call, but…"

"No!" Alfie shook her head. "We're sticking together. And I'm not letting Elsea out of my sight. I don't want anything to happen to her, even though she caused us problems. I'd never forgive myself."

Elsea gasped and started crying again as she said, "Thank you. I don't want to be left here with a killer on the loose. I don't deserve a cousin like you."

The three young ladies decided to remain in the house together. Every step they took seemed too loud, but the house remained silent and still.

Deloris went back to the phone and picked up the receiver. After a minute, the operator answered. Deloris apologized for the late-night call but explained that there was an emergency and she needed to speak to the Daviess County sheriff. The call was put through, and the sheriff answered. He remembered working with Deloris on the bandstand murder and knew when she called it was a genuine emergency. He apologized for not coming earlier, but he'd just returned to the station and hadn't picked up his messages. Once she'd explained the urgency, he said he would be there in about twenty-two minutes.

The girls sat in the living room and waited for the sheriff to arrive. Deloris looked out the window at the body again. One arm was thrown over the face, but the mouth and beard looked familiar.

The sheriff and his deputy arrived in separate cars. Deloris and Alfie gave their statements to the sheriff while the deputy hand-cuffed Elsea and put her in his squad car. When he returned, the deputy and the sheriff searched the house. While they were search-ing, the local funeral home director, who served as the county coroner when needed, drove up in his van. The sheriff and his deputy didn't find anyone in the house or the outbuildings, so there wasn't much else they could do. The deputy took Elsea away in his car, while the sheriff and the coroner prepared to load the body into the van. Alfie turned away as they carried the body off of the porch, but Deloris kept watch. When she saw his face fully, she knew who he was; it was the man who had tried to stop them on the bridge. The coroner drove away with the body, and the sheriff returned to the front porch.

"It's Wilbur Whetstone," Deloris said.

"Yes, 'tis," the sheriff replied.

"How did he end up here? Like this?" Alfie asked. "We saw him Friday while we were driving in from Pattonsburg."

"Don't reckon I know. But we'll do some poking around, see what we can figure out," the sheriff told Alfie. "For now, let me drive you two home."

Sunday, November 1, 1942

Before breakfast the next morning, Deloris called a friend in Kansas City and asked her to cover for her at her job at the police switchboard on Monday and Tuesday. Deloris smiled as she hung up the phone and assured Alfie that she had permission to stay for two more days. Then Alfie and Deloris ate breakfast and went to church. Everyone in the congregation detained them after the church service, asking for details about what had happened the previous night.

When they could finally say their goodbyes, they headed out in Alfie's car to Deloris's parents' house for Sunday dinner. The Markhams lived on a farm a few miles outside of Jameson, and Deloris would have been in big trouble if she hadn't stopped in to say hello to Momma and Dad.

"How did everyone find out so quickly about the murder?" Alfie asked as they drove away.

"I believe it was Mrs. Martin, the telephone operator," Deloris explained. "Remember, she knows everything that goes on in Jameson and that I do detective work in Kansas City?"

"Oh, that's right, she's who you spoke to last night."

"Of course, it could also be the sheriff, or his deputy, or the coroner, or the sheriff's wife. Or all of them telling the story to their friends simultaneously."

"Goodness, I didn't think about all of them knowing, but I guess I thought it would take a little longer for the story to get out," Alfie agreed.

Sunday dinner was as delicious as always with light hot rolls and burnt sugar cake, but, while Deloris loved her family and was happy to see them, she also knew that she and Alfie still needed to go back to the house and finish the search for the ring. And, Deloris thought, now she also wanted to solve the murder. So, she hugged her parents tight and headed out right after the meal, not lingering to chat as she usually did. Besides, they still had most of the family there and were busy visiting with them.

"Are you still up for searching the attic?" Alfie asked as she pointed the car toward town.

"Of course," Deloris replied.

Alfie and Deloris arrived in Jameson and drove directly to the house of Alfie's grandmother. By tacit agreement, they entered the house through the back door, avoiding the front entryway. They were armed with the same implements they carried last night, with Deloris wielding the cast iron frying pan and Alfie clutching the rolling pin and flashlight. They had put them in the car this morning before going to church. Imagine what everyone would think of their arsenal, Deloris had commented. As they went up the narrow stairs to the attic, the second step creaked, and Deloris stopped abruptly.

"That step has always creaked," Alfie said. "No one ever bothered to fix it, I guess."

"I see," Deloris said as she looked down at the step and pushed her foot up and down on it. "I could try to fix it before I leave."

Once in the attic, they saw humpback steamer trunks, flat top steamer trunks, huge wardrobe travel trunks, wooden boxes stacked one upon another, a baby highchair, and various pieces of old broken furniture. Old hats hung on a coat rack, and old pictures and a mirror hung precariously on the walls.

"Your family must have done a lot of traveling with all of these steamer trunks?" Deloris asked.

"My grandparents traveled all over Europe, Africa, and Asia in their younger years."

"Which trunk did you find the important papers?"

"That one over there in the corner."

"Let's start looking in the two steamer trunks there," Deloris suggested, intrigued by what might be found. "You search this trunk and I'll search the other one, or vice versa, if you prefer."

The steamer trunk Deloris opened had boxes full of quilting material in the bottom, and the compartments in the top were full of thread, yarn, and darning needles. Underneath them were various women's magazines, from the late 1800s to early 1900s. The trunk that Alfie opened had family pictures and albums filling it to the brim, along with letters from family and friends through the years. A quill pen, ink, and writing paper were in a small box underneath the pictures. Deloris moved on to one of the wardrobe trunks and, with Alfie's help, they sat it up on one end to open it. When Deloris discovered it was upside down, they turned it the other way around. Deloris helped Alfie with the other one and, luckily, they guessed the correct side up the first time.

Inside the wardrobe trunk were three women's dresses from the mid to late 19th century along with petticoats. One dress was black, obviously for a widow to wear, with the veil found in a drawer on the right. Another dress was for formal affairs and the third was more of an everyday functional type. On the other side in the drawers, she found pantaloons, stockings, and corsets all neatly folded. Deloris removed the dresses and undergarments and carefully placed them on a wooden box nearby. Underneath all the dresses were two pairs of high-top boots.

"Look at this," Alfie encouraged her to come to the flat top trunk she opened.

There was a Civil War uniform for the Union army, neatly folded and stacked inside. Laying across the top of the uniform was an officer's sword, scabbard, and hat.

"This is so exciting," Alfie exclaimed. "This must be my four-times great-grandfather's uniform."

She removed the sword and scabbard and placed them on the floor. Then she carefully removed the uniform and placed it on one of the wooden boxes. She then removed all the other items and articles of clothing to search the nooks and crannies of that trunk but met with no success.

Deloris returned to the trunk and ran her fingers around the inside. Not finding a hidden compartment, she started to put the boots back inside the trunk when on a whim she decided to try the boots on. Before she put them on, she put her hand inside the left boot to make sure nothing like a spider was inside. She felt something in the toe of the boot and cautiously pulled out a hand-embroidered lace handkerchief that was wrapped around something small. The lace was starting to fall apart, so she slowly and carefully opened each layer.

"Hey, I found something," she said excitedly.

Alfie stopped what she was doing and ran over to Deloris. "What is it? Unwrap it!"

"I'm trying to be careful, but it is wrapped so tightly, and the lace is crumbling in my hands."

"Don't worry about the lace. Just open it," Alfie anxiously exclaimed.

Unwrapped, the handkerchief revealed a gold locket with a picture of a man wearing the same uniform they found in the other trunk.

"This is so much fun, Alfie. It is like a treasure hunt."

"It's a treasure I wasn't expecting," Alfie smiled. "That must be a picture of my four-times great-grandfather."

"Yes, but unfortunately, it isn't the ring. Don't give up yet. We'll keep looking."

Deloris and Alfie had just returned to their searches when they heard something fall with a loud crash in the kitchen. Deloris and Alfie froze in fright.

"Do you think there could be someone else still searching for the ring and they killed Wilbur?"

"I don't know," Alfie said, "but it is possible that Elsea's sister could be here. Or Uncle Earl's sons. But Elsea didn't mention anyone else last night. Plus, I really don't think my relatives are murderers."

Deloris didn't say anything, but if Alfie's relatives hadn't murdered the man last night, who did? Elsea had been in the house before Deloris and Alfie arrived. Someone with her could have killed Wilbur and left the body on the front porch before they began searching for the ring. And why had Elsea, or whoever the murderer was, left him on Alfie's grandmother's front porch?

"You stay up here and continue searching," Deloris said. "I'll go investigate."

"No way am I letting you go alone," Alfie insisted. "I know you are fearless and all, but you don't need to always investigate alone and put yourself in danger all the time, and especially not after last night."

Alfie picked up the rolling pin and Deloris led the way with the frying pan. As they descended, they could hear other items falling in the kitchen. The same step creaked again as they went down the stairs, and whoever was in the kitchen must have heard the creak, because the noise stopped.

Cautiously creeping, they arrived at the kitchen just in time to see a black cat dash outside through a tear in the back screen door. There was a glass bowl in pieces on the floor, and several cooking utensils were scattered around an overturned crock.

"Oh, heavens!" said Alfie, caught between laughter and fright.

"I have an idea," Deloris said, as she went back towards the attic. Alfie followed her. When they got to the attic stairs, Deloris climbed up to the squeaky step. Then she sat down on the step below and examined the noisy tread. There was a large crack at the back of the step, and when she shined the flashlight at it, she saw a glint of metal. It looked like a small hinge. Looking at the other side of the crack, she saw one there, too. "Alfie, come here. Look at this. Did you ever notice these hinges tucked into this step before?"

"No."

Deloris curled her fingers under the front of the tread and pulled upward. The board raised to reveal a secret compartment. Alfie gasped. The compartment was mostly empty, but an envelope was propped in a corner. Deloris handed the letter to Alfie, who sat down beside her and opened it, with Deloris peering over her shoulder.

"It's my grandmother's handwriting."

"What does it say?"

"Love that is handed down for generations will always shine on. It needs no flowers; it is written in stone." Alfie paused. "Huh."

"It's a clue," Deloris said. "'Shine on' and 'handed down generations' are referring to the ring, for sure."

"But what about the rest?"

"I'm not sure," Deloris replied, wrinkling her brow in thought.

"Can we think about it at home? I believe we've searched pretty much everywhere we can here."

"Of course. We'll take the letter back to your place. Maybe there are additional clues, like something written in onion juice that can only be seen if you heat the paper," Deloris said with a chuckle.

Back in Alfie's kitchen, they were still examining the paper, though they hadn't found anything new when the sheriff knocked on Alfie's door and said he had news.

"Yes?" Alfie asked cautiously, standing at the door.

"May I come in?"

"Yes, certainly, Sheriff."

"You said last night you saw Wilbur Whetstone on Friday evening?"

"Yes. I'd just picked up Deloris from the bus station in Pattonsburg. We were driving back to Jameson, and he jumped out at us by the bridge over Big Creek.

"Interesting," the sheriff replied. "I'm trying to find the last time anyone saw him alive besides the murderer, of course, and so far, you two are it. But Wilbur didn't have a car. I suppose he coulda walked all the way from Pattonsburg to Jameson, but I'm not sure why he would."

"Do you have any leads on why he would have been in Jameson and why he was killed?" Deloris asked.

The sheriff shook his head. "He's made enough people angry. I wouldn't be surprised if someone took a potshot at him, but someone stabbed him in the back. That's not a scare-you-away-with-birdshot type of accidental death. Someone meant to do this. Please don't go back to your grandmother's house, especially at night, until we find the person who did this."

"I won't," Alfie promised, "and I'll call Mrs. O'Casey and ask her to keep an eye on the house."

"Good idea. Tell her to call me if she sees anything there."

"But we need to still find the item we've been looking for," Deloris said as she nudged Alfie. "We need to go back to the house to look."

"Oh, yes, sir. We do need to go back to the house," Alfie added. "But I will call Mrs. O'Casey."

"Okay, then. Just be careful and if you see anything out of the ordinary, anything at all, call me," the sheriff insisted.

Once the sheriff left, Alfie called Lara O'Casey, sharing the receiver with Deloris so that they could both talk. Lara had already heard about all the events of Saturday night through the neighborhood gossip, and she promised she'd let the sheriff know if she saw anything out of the ordinary. "But it's been very quiet," Lara said. "I saw you girls drive up to the house after lunch, and the only thing I've seen at all this afternoon were two tractors and a traveling salesman driving down the road."

After talking to Lara, Alfie and Deloris made dinner, a hearty vegetable and potato stew. As they were washing dishes, they continued talking about what the letter might mean. Alfie suggested that flowers might mean the flower gardens outside of the house, and they agreed to search there tomorrow. But neither Alfie nor Deloris could figure out what the stone might be.

"Maybe a limestone fence post?" Alfie suggested.

"Or the basement of the house? It's made of stone?"

"No, we already looked down there. There's no writing on the stone walls, just cobwebs and probably rats."

"That's true. It needs to have writing. The letter said written in stone," Deloris said. Suddenly, she stopped washing the dish she was holding. Alfie looked at her questioningly. "Flowers and stones. And words."

"Yes?"

Deloris snapped her fingers, getting spatters of soapy water on both of them, exclaiming, "That's it! An engraved stone. With flowers. It's a gravestone."

"Oh!" Alfie said. "My four-times great-grandparents' graves are in the Jameson cemetery. It's a double headstone, and there's an urn we put flowers in on Memorial Day."

"Let's go!" said Deloris. "I want to look inside that urn."

Though Alfie was not excited about heading to the cemetery after dark, Deloris convinced her to try.

"Why do we have to do this at night? Can't we wait until tomorrow?"

"Don't you want me to help you find the ring? Remember, I only have two days off from work."

Alfie resigned herself to going that night but was also excited to see if their hunch was correct.

They retrieved the flashlight, frying pan, and rolling pin and set out in Alfie's car. The cemetery was a mile outside of town, and when they parked and Alfie turned the headlights off, the moon provided them with just enough light for them to see.

Alfie turned on the flashlight and led the way to the gravestone, clasping her rolling pin, but all was quiet. When they got there, she pointed the light at the front of the double headstone, illuminating a small urn that was turned upside down and halfway buried in the soil. Deloris cautiously pulled it out and turned it over, hoping against hope that no snake, spider, or mouse had made the urn its home. But nothing ran out and attacked her fingers.

"Shine the light in the urn, please, so I can see if there is anything in there before I put my hand in there," she asked Alfie. "I can just barely see that there is something inside at the bottom."

When she put her hand into the urn, she felt something wrapped in a cloth with what she thought was a small, hard box inside. It was jammed in the bottom so tightly she had to really work to get it out. She succeeded in taking a hold of a corner of the cloth and pulled the package out. She then handed it to Alfie. It was small and wrapped securely in oilcloth. Alfie unwrapped the cloth to reveal a box, black with a gilt text that read: Whetstone Jewelry,

Jameson, Missouri. With trembling fingers, Alfie opened it to find a small, black velvet bag. Alfie loosened the drawstrings and turned the bag upside down. Out fell a handkerchief, and when Alfie unwrapped the handkerchief, there it was: her grandmother's ring! The sapphires and diamonds glittered in the flashlight's beam.

"We found it!" Alfie exclaimed. "I'm so happy, Deloris. This means so much to me. Thank you for helping me retrieve the ring."

"Of course! I'm just so glad we found it!" Alfie put the ring on her finger, and Deloris frowned. "Please be careful that someone doesn't rob you of it. I suggest you hide it and pretend you are still looking for it to throw anyone off of robbing you. At least until you can get it into a safe deposit box."

"That's a good idea," Alfie said, and she put the ring back in the box and tucked the box securely into her pocket.

Alfie and Deloris drove back home and when they got inside, Alfie took the ring out of the box to look at it again in better light. It sparkled and shone. After they spent some time admiring it, Deloris picked up the ring box to hand to Alfie so she could put the ring away, but then she stopped and stared at the jeweler's name printed on the box.

"What was the man's name who was killed? Wasn't it Wilbur Whetstone?" she asked.

"Yes, that's right."

"And you said he worked in his father's store. Was that store Whetstone Jewelry?" Alfie nodded, and Deloris showed her the ring box. Alfie's eyes got big, and Deloris said, "There are no secrets in small towns, and his father was the jeweler. I'll bet you an apple pie that Wilbur Whetstone knew all about your grandmother's ring when his father cleaned it and fixed the prong."

"I believe you, Deloris, and maybe that's why Wilbur was at my grandmother's house, but who killed Wilbur?"

"I don't know," Deloris replied, "but I intend to find out."

Monday, November 2, 1942

The next morning over breakfast, Alfie asked Deloris what the plan was for the day. Deloris explained that she wanted to call the sheriff, to find out if he'd discovered anyone else who'd seen or talked to Wilbur on Friday or Saturday. Alfie agreed, and once the breakfast dishes had been cleared, Deloris phoned the sheriff's office. The sheriff wasn't in, and the deputy told her he'd gone to Pattonsburg. He offered to come by and showed up at Alfie's house fifteen minutes later. Deloris thanked the deputy for his help on Saturday evening and told him she appreciated his professionalism. She then told him that he looked "so handsome and strong in his uniform."

"Thank you, ma'am. Happy to help." He put his head down and blushed a little.

"You don't have to call me ma'am. You can call me Deloris."

After buttering him up some, she asked him why the sheriff had gone to Pattonsburg, and the deputy, making her promise not to tell anyone, said that the sheriff was tracking down a possibility that Wilbur had stayed in the hotel there on Friday night. The sheriff talked to one of the individuals he knew who often fed

Wilbur, and that person told the sheriff that he drove Wilbur to the hotel in Pattonsburg late Friday night.

"Deloris, we need to go," Alfie said, slightly embarrassed at her friend's comments, and pushed her toward the kitchen. She then turned to say goodbye and thank you to the officer and closed the door. Once the deputy left, she turned to Deloris and said, "What are you doing? You're a married woman."

"I was just getting information," she said with a wry smile.

On a hunch, Deloris placed a call to the Pattonsburg hotel and asked for the sheriff. When he came on the line, the sheriff grumbled about his deputy revealing too much information, but he answered Deloris's question, telling her that the overnight desk clerk had looked at a photo of Wilbur and confirmed that a man who looked like that had stayed there Friday evening.

"Did anyone else stay in the hotel that night?" Deloris asked.

"Just a salesman and some relatives visiting for a christening. I'm going to speak with them all and ask if they knew Wilbur."

Deloris promised to let him go back to his conversation with the clerk but requested that he let her know if he found anything out, and he said he would.

As she hung up the phone, Deloris thought about the guests at the hotel and then turned to Alfie, who'd only heard one side of the conversation. "Do you remember—did Lara O'Casey say what kind of traveling salesman came by her place?"

Alfie shook her head no, but then picked up the phone and called Lara. A quick conversation later, she hung up the phone, turned to Deloris, and said, "It was a knife salesman. He had all kinds, Lara said, from paring knives up to cleavers."

Deloris grabbed the phone and, to the exasperation of the operator, placed another call to the hotel in Pattonsburg. She got the front desk clerk, insisted on speaking to the sheriff again, and told the clerk to say that it was urgent.

A few minutes later, the sheriff picked up and said, "Deloris, I said I'd keep you posted, but I have to finish talking to everyone here first. Let me do my job."

Deloris ignored the complaint. "Sheriff, Mrs. O'Casey mentioned seeing a traveling salesman on Sunday," Deloris continued, "and when we were driving to Jameson the night we saw Wilbur, we passed a truck headed to Pattonsburg. There was a logo on the side."

"That's all circumstantial... but worth looking into. Thanks."

"There's more—Alfie just spoke to Lara; she said it was a knife salesman that she saw. And didn't you say Wilbur was stabbed?"

There was a pause, and then the sheriff said, "Good work, Deloris. I was just about to speak to the salesman here. The clerk says he's up in his room. I think it's the same man. His truck is out front, advertising the sale and sharpening of knives. I'm going to call the Pattonsburg deputy, and we'll round him up." The sheriff hung up abruptly.

Deloris and Alfie were on tenterhooks for the next hour, waiting for the phone to ring. When it finally did, they both ran for it, but Deloris used her hip to nudge Alfie out of the way so that she could grab the receiver first. Then Alfie nudged back and said, "My phone." Deloris moved over and they shared the receiver so they both could hear.

The sheriff told them that the traveling salesman had been arrested for the murder of Wilbur Whetstone. A search of his truck had found spatters of blood and a knife that matched the wound that had caused Wilbur's death. Once confronted with the evidence, the salesman confessed. He'd picked Wilbur up on the road Friday night and Wilbur had told him he was going to Jameson and told him about the ring. "Wilbur never did have a lick of sense. Why would he tell a total stranger about the ring?" the sheriff exclaimed.

The sheriff continued, explaining that the salesman said he agreed to help Wilbur search for the ring, but when they got there, they saw all of the lights in the house going on and off. The salesman wanted to leave, but Wilbur was going to break in anyway even though there were people inside. He planned to rob them, and those people inside were you. The salesman tried to reason with him, but when Wilbur walked up to the front door, the salesman panicked and stabbed him. He heard Alfie and Deloris confront Elsea in the shed at the back, at which point he got scared and snuck away, with no one the wiser. He figured he would lie low until things cooled down and return to look for the ring.

The sheriff ended the call by saying, "I appreciate your help, Deloris. Might not have caught him without you."

As soon as the receiver was back in the cradle, Deloris and Alfie started jumping in celebration. "You did it!" Alfie crowed. Deloris just grinned from ear to ear.

A little while later, the two young ladies carefully walked the ring over to the Jameson Farmers Bank, where Alfie put it into her safe deposit box. Deloris and Alfie each told a different teller that the ring had been found and was safely stored, so that word would get around Jameson and no one else would try to break into the house to find it.

As they left the bank, Deloris said, "You can't keep a secret in a small town, but you sure can pass information out to your benefit."

"You're absolutely right," Alfie agreed. "And thank you again for all your help. Let's go back to the house and get something to eat, then I can drive you back to Pattonsburg so you can catch the afternoon bus back to Kansas City."

Deloris nodded and gave her friend a big hug. Though they were sad that their time together was too short, the friends vowed to meet up again before spring.

Juliet E. Sidonie

If you liked this cozy mystery set in 1942, you can read more about Deloris's adventures as an amateur sleuth in *Murder Among Friends*, where you'll step into the glamorous world of 1930s Kansas City. Befriending reporters, police officers, and everyone in-between, feisty Miss Markham proves there's no such thing as an unsolvable mystery when she's around! This fun-filled mystery is inspired by true-life historical events and characters. Learn more at MissMarkhamMysteries.com.

Chapter Five

Holt Jacobs and the Halloween Splash

Lily Stirling

I frowned at one of the loudspeakers.

"Monster Mash."

Again.

I'd been the lifeguard for twenty-three minutes, and I swear the Halloween playlist had three songs on repeat: "The Addams Family," "Ghostbusters," and "Monster Mash."

How could anyone stand it? It was one thing to try to set a tone, but surely there were plenty of other spooky songs.

Cauldrons had been borrowed from the theater department. They were filled with dry ice and placed around the indoor pool, giving the whole area a misty, almost spooky look, which made watching the water a little trickier. Lucky for me, everyone was in costume, and so far no one had even dipped a toe in the water.

A man's voice drifted over the sounds of the party. "...when the building was unlocked in the morning, the body of a woman was found floating in the water."

I'd begun massaging my temples even before the excited gasps. The Drowned Girl. Always the Drowned Girl.

It didn't matter who told the story. It remained more or less unchanged. Our campus pool had closed, and the next morning there was a murdered college-aged woman floating on the surface. Supposedly, the building for the indoor pool was locked up tight. There wasn't any key card use during the time of death, and they never identified the woman.

"…the lifeguards will never admit it, but"—I squeezed my eyes shut. The guy was ramping up to the *best* part—"sometimes they'll hear her calling for help or see her struggling in the water. But once they dive in, she disappears."

Unbelievable. The whole story was unbelievable. As far as I knew, no one had ever drowned in the campus pool. And you'd think if a murderer were drowning mysterious women, there'd be some actual evidence, like newspaper articles or police reports.

My eyes were trained on the pool—like a good lifeguard—so I didn't notice the figure approaching me.

"Holt, you're working? I thought Sean was on duty."

If today weren't Halloween and I hadn't been the official lifeguard for *Ghouls by the Pool: A Halloween Costume Party*, I would have jumped at the sight of the man by my lifeguard station. Even then, my eyes got pretty wide.

The guy's name was Marcus. He usually looked like your average college pretty boy, but tonight he was split into two distinct halves. His right side had hair stylishly slicked back, and he wore half a white lab coat and carried a leather bag. On the left side, he wore an old-timey coat, with wild hair, dark circles under his eye, and a scar painted along his cheek.

"Dr. Jekyll and Mr. Hyde," Marcus said when all I did was stare at him.

"Got it," I said.

Costumes were mandatory for entering the party—though some people definitely put more effort into it than others.

I'm not big on costumes, but tonight's uniform was a zip-up Baywatch sweatshirt, which I'd worn with a pair of black swim trunks. As the party's official lifeguard, I needed to be able to move should there be an emergency.

Baywatch wasn't my first choice, but Sean had already bought the sweatshirt, so it was the easiest option. Plus, my shoulder-length hair vaguely resembled David Hasselhoff's hair in the eighties.

Marcus asked, "Why are you working this instead of Sean?"

"Sean was supposed to." There was a hint of exasperation in my voice. "But he got asked to do a swim race for charity, so I'm covering the first two hours."

"Is that the fundraiser for kids cancer, where all the swimmers are dressed as superheroes and have to compete with capes on?"

I shrugged. How was I supposed to know?

"And you?" I asked. "Why are you here?" We weren't exactly friends, but we'd paired up for a few engineering assignments. "Shouldn't you be somewhere with more adult beverages?"

Maybe it was a rude question given I didn't know Marcus very well. Yet he didn't seem the type to be at a campus-sponsored, alcohol-free Halloween party. Since I'd started college, I'd never attended Ghouls by the Pool, and the only reason I was here tonight was as a paid favor.

Aside from the cauldrons of dry ice, the decorations were pretty cheesy. Fake cobwebby stuff stretched across the diving blocks and the lifeguard stations, with a *tasteful* number of plastic spiders added. The back wall was lined with carved jack-o'-lanterns glowing with fake candles.

It was a party catering to freshmen and students who wanted a party but not a *party*. However, there was also a tradition that involved trying to spike the punch, which was why the school hired a college student to supervise the snack station. Everyone knew that *supervise the snack station* was code for making sure the punch remained alcohol-free.

This year the snack supervisor was a woman who'd gone overboard with a vampire look. Which I guess worked. It didn't matter it was a costume. No one wants to start a fight with a vampire.

"Why am I at the party?" Marcus repeated like he didn't know the answer. "Uhh...I was kind of dared to be here." Marcus fidgeted with the Dr. Jekyll side of his collar, while his eyes darted around the room. "You know how it is."

I gave a noncommittal "Okay" since, as a general rule, I don't believe in doing weird stuff just because someone dared me to.

Wait. No way all Marcus had to do was *attend* Ghouls by the Pool. Was he in charge of spiking the punch this year? Or was he the one telling the stories about the Drowned Girl?

"So, what?" I asked. "Are you just supposed to hang out here instead of party with your friends?"

Marcus's eyes shot past me, and then he frowned. His attention shifted back to me. "What? Er, yeah, I guess." Again, his gaze moved from me, and he mumbled something about needing to talk to someone.

I checked the massive clock on the wall across from me. One hour and thirty-two minutes until Sean relieved me. Hopefully, the only part of Marcus's dare was *attending* a campus-sponsored Halloween party. I didn't want to deal with any Halloween tricks during my two hours on duty.

"Would you like some punch?"

The woman's voice surprised me. For the second time, I'd been too focused on the pool to pay attention to the Halloween partiers.

I would have grinned and said something charming, except the voice sounded familiar...too familiar. Sure enough, the person dressed in ripped jeans, a football jersey, and eye black under both eyes like a professional football player wasn't a college student. It was my baby sister.

"Juniper!"

Instinctively, I looked at the guys around us, most of them watching her. At my scowl, the majority of them looked away.

"Why are you here?" I asked. When I lived at home, Juniper would try to tag along on anything she thought might be exciting, but this was her first time crashing my university.

"Hello, Holt. Good to see you too." Juniper batted her eyes like she wasn't guilty of sneaking onto campus.

"Why are you at my college?" I snapped, giving a death glare to a guy who had been looking at Juniper too long.

Unlike half the students at the party, my sister was at least covered completely by her costume. The problem was that Juniper could cast a spell on almost anyone, and the guys here would think she was over eighteen.

"I came to see you."

"Juniper..." I shook my head. How had I forgotten how frustrating she could be? "You're not old enough to be here. And college guys are creeps."

"You're a college guy."

"And you've called me a creep." I sighed. "How did you even get here?"

Juniper tossed her hair. "I drove."

"You have a license?"

"Yeah." She rolled her eyes. "I've had a license for a super-long time."

I raised an eyebrow. While I'm never quite sure the age of either of my sisters, there's no way Juniper was old enough to have had her driver's license for a *super-long* time.

"Would you relax?" Juniper said.

"You're not supposed to be here!" I looked away from her to check the pool. "Does Mom know?"

"Eh"—Juniper waved her hand—"don't worry about Mom."

Don't worry about Mom?

My baby sister had driven for hours by herself and snuck into my college campus's Halloween pool party. If anything happened, Mom would blame me.

"Where do Mom and Dad think you are?" I asked.

Juniper rolled her eyes. For some reason, she hadn't considered me going full overprotective older brother if she showed up at my school. "Mom's gone this weekend giving a guest lecture, and I told Dad I was seeing a friend."

"A friend?"

Juniper raised one shoulder. "Siblings can be friends."

My jaw ticked. "When Mom figures this out—and she will figure it out—you'll be grounded until you graduate from high school."

"Why would I be grounded?" Juniper argued. "I'm here doing a good deed."

My attention was caught by the loud laughter of a group of guys dressed like hockey players. They were roughhousing, but so far it was all lighthearted, and no one was being pushed into the pool.

"What good deed?" I asked when I finally glanced back at Juniper.

"Mom said you and Tasha broke up. I thought you'd like someone to hold your hand as you ate ice cream and watched cheesy movies."

All I did was raise an eyebrow. Sure, I'd gotten dumped, but I wasn't about to cry into a tub of ice cream.

"None of that sounds like me."

"But you're clearly upset," Juniper said. "You're spending Halloween at a pool party."

"You don't know what I'm like at college."

Juniper poked my shoulder. "But I know you. And you would never voluntarily attend a party."

"I'm *working*. Not *attending*."

"Whatever. My point is you definitely had a date planned. And now you're single, working some campus-sponsored pool event. Sounds like you could use a friend."

Whoa. There was so much there to respond to. Sure, she'd correctly guessed that I'd originally planned to be on a date right now, but she made it sound like I don't *have* friends...which I do.

I was about to answer when a scream had my head snapping away from Juniper to the far side of the pool. A woman dressed as a 1920s flapper girl was stumbling and waving her arms wildly at the pool's edge.

"Help her!" I yelled. But a second later there was a splash as she fell into the deep end.

"It's the Drowned Girl!" someone shouted.

First off: No, just no.

Second off: Ghosts don't make a splash.

I began striding toward the spot where she'd fallen. I expected Flapper Girl to pop up any moment, and all I'd need to do was give her a hand out of the pool. But she remained under the water, and the only thing to rise to the surface was Flapper Girl's peacock-feather headband.

The pool was so long, and the party was so crowded, that I wasn't getting there fast enough. Flapper Girl was still moving, yet for some reason, she wasn't rising to the surface for more air.

I needed to reach her, but everyone was too busy staring at her to get out of my way. There was only one clear path, so I chucked my Baywatch sweatshirt and dove into the water. Now, in case you're wondering, I could still see Flapper Girl in the water. And according to legend, the Drowned Girl disappeared the moment anyone got in the water to rescue her.

I began swimming toward her. But I needed to be faster. In high school, I was part of the swim team. But since starting college, I'd quit the swim team to focus on my engineering degree, and all the speed I'd worked so hard for was no longer in my muscle memory.

My eyes burned as I tried to see in the chlorinated water without goggles. Flapper Girl's movements were slowing, and she had to be running out of air.

Come on. I had to move faster.

When I'd almost reached her, I took one deep inhale before diving to the bottom.

As a lifeguard, you're trained over and over on what to do if a drowning person panics and tries to fight you. Flapper Girl didn't fight. But she was a solid flesh and blood human (not a ghost). I couldn't tell if she was conscious. After getting my arms under her armpits, I pushed off from the bottom of the pool, and we shot up to the surface.

I took a deep inhale, but I couldn't feel Flapper Girl breathing. She needed some real first aid.

My hair was loose, covering my eyes, and I shook my head back to get it out of my face.

"Can you hear me?" I practically shouted as I began paddling the two of us to the side of the pool. The party had gone silent—except for "Ghostbusters" playing in the background—and my words echoed around the room.

Flapper Girl didn't answer.

The guys dressed as hockey players were waiting at the edge and helped lift her out of the water.

"Watch her head!" I yelled as her neck rolled and her skull almost collided with the cement.

"Got it," one of the guys said, supporting her head just in time.

I was out of the water a second later. I had to check for a pulse and see if she was breathing.

It was okay. I could do this. I was certified in first aid. Sure, I'd only practiced on test dummies in the past, but it was fine. This was what I'd trained for.

Flapper Girl's pulse was strong, but she wasn't breathing.

A pulse meant *don't* do CPR...right? *Only* do rescue breaths but keep checking and if the pulse stops, begin CPR.

I pinched her nose and was just getting her mouth open when Flapper Girl coughed up water, and her eyes fluttered open.

It's probably bad that the first wave of relief I felt was because I didn't need to attempt a rescue breath.

"Are you okay?" I asked. "Can you hear me?"

But I couldn't even hear myself because once Flapper Girl began moving, the whole party erupted with cheers and people talking over one another in their excitement.

Flapper Girl's eyes darted around like she didn't know where she was. I bent close and accidentally dripped water on her face. "What's your name?"

Her eyes finally focused on mine. "Me?"

"Yes," I said. "What's your name?"

"Rachel."

"Well, Rachel"—I gave my best comforting smile—"my name is Holt."

"Nice to meet you," she said instinctively, before wiping water from her face and smearing her makeup.

"Did you hit your head?" I asked, battling a strange urge to feel her scalp.

"Um..." Rachel half sat up and lightly touched her forehead. "I don't think so." She gave a few weak coughs, but instead of relaxing back against the cement, she mustered up the energy to sit up all the way.

Someone dressed as a princess descended on Rachel the Flapper Girl with a large beach towel. "Here, put this on before you start shaking."

"Thank you," Rachel said quietly.

"I'll call 911," the princess said.

Rachel's eyebrows shot up. "Don't." She gave a shaky laugh. "I'm fine. Or great. No need to bother them."

I shared a worried look with her friend. "It is protocol for an ambulance to come when there's been a—" I almost said, *drowning*, but thankfully stopped myself. "Been an accident."

"But if they came here, I could refuse their help?"

"Yeah, I guess so."

She shrugged. "Well, I would refuse, so there's no need to bother them."

I shook my head. "But with the way you sank in the water, you must have a head injury." I sort of reached toward her, but she scooted back on the cement.

"I didn't hit anything," she said. "One of my shoes was loose, and I tripped." She gestured to where she'd fallen, and there, like a vibrant blue version of Cinderella's slipper, was her shoe lying sideways at the pool's edge.

"Okay," I said slowly. "But if that's why you fell, why did you sink to the bottom?"

There would have been an awkward silence if my teenage sister hadn't whisper-shouted, "Holt!" like I was embarrassing her.

"Sorry, that came out wrong," I said. "I only meant, why—"

"Rachel needs to rest now," her princess friend announced, then widened her eyes at Rachel. Presumably friend code for *This guy is a college creep.*

"Gotcha," I said. I stood up, then remembered to ask, "You're sure you don't want an ambulance?"

Rachel was drying her face off with the towel, streaking her already running makeup even more. "I'm sure."

I was going to grab the shoe that was resting by the pool when I noticed Rachel's feet were missing both shoes. When I didn't spot the second shoe near the first, I checked the pool.

The other vibrant blue heel was resting at the very bottom. I had to fight the urge to tell Rachel she needed footwear that would stay on her feet. I stayed silent and walked to the pool's edge, only to stare down at her shoe.

Maybe I shouldn't complain, but I almost never got into the water while on duty, and I wasn't even supposed to be working tonight.

I took a deep breath and dove back into the pool to retrieve the bright blue heel from the bottom. And here's the thing, I *dove* because water is buoyant and likes to hold you up. There was no good reason for Flapper Girl to sink to the very bottom...unless it was intentional.

Once I'd grabbed the shoe, there was also the peacock-feather headband, but at least that had the decency to float gently on the surface. I swam to the edge of the pool, where Flapper Girl's other shoe was resting. It was like she'd tripped out of one shoe only to tumble into the water.

Still, why had she sunk? Was it pure panic that kept her down there? Or had she been waiting to be rescued?

But why?

That didn't make sense. Still, what were the chances of tripping out of a shoe, plummeting headfirst into the deep end of a pool, and then making no effort to push up out of the water?

"Do you need a hand?" My sister's voice surprised me. She was crouching at the edge in her football jersey, watching me curiously.

Juniper had probably caught me staring off into space. I was in the water, still clutching one shoe and the peacock hairpiece. "I'm good," I said before climbing onto the cement.

I returned both shoes and the peacock thing to Rachel, who was now surrounded by a group of friends. "You're sure you don't need an ambulance?" I asked.

Rachel nodded. "I promise I'm fine. Just embarrassed."

"All right."

Strange thing about saving someone's life during a Halloween party—the party keeps going.

I left Rachel the Flapper Girl with her friends. While I'd feel better if she got checked out, it wasn't like I could force her. So I returned to the lifeguard station and got my towel, which somehow had gotten a mass of fake cobwebs stuck to it. Once I'd removed the cobwebs, I started drying off my shoulder-length hair, since it kept dripping onto my chest.

"You know," Juniper said, "people thought Rachel was the Drowned Girl, coming back to haunt the party."

I shook my head. "People were expecting an actual ghoul by the pool?"

Juniper gasped. "So you've heard about the Drowned Girl? Did you know her body was never identified?" Juniper sounded wayyy too excited. "She was buried as a Jane Doe."

"Of course, *I* know about the Drowned Girl. How do *you* know about her? You don't even go to school here."

"That Dr. Jekyll guy told me when I was getting our punch."

Marcus? Did Marcus crash a freshman party to tell ghost stories?

"Were you going to kiss her?" Juniper asked.

"What?"

Juniper's question came out of nowhere.

I pulled away the towel so I could look at Juniper. "Who?"

"Rachel," she said.

"Ew, no."

"Ew?" Juniper raised her eyebrows. "What do you mean *ew*?"

Yikes. I'd really messed up. Juniper was here because she was sure I was devastated about my breakup. If I told my sister I wasn't ready to kiss anyone whose name wasn't Tasha, she'd get these big puppy-dog eyes and say, *Aww, Holt.*

That couldn't happen. So I went on the defense. "When Rachel wasn't breathing, I was about to give her a rescue breath. Ever heard of one? That's way different from kissing."

But Juniper was no longer paying attention to me. Instead, she was looking around the lifeguard station with raised eyebrows. I don't know. Maybe she was distracted by a fake spider on the cobwebs.

I had just wrapped the towel around my waist and was putting on my Baywatch sweatshirt when Juniper said, "Um, Holt..." and bit her lip.

What had she done?

"Yeah?" I asked, my voice holding older-sibling superiority.

"Well"—Juniper wouldn't look at me—"my wallet's missing."

"Missing?" I squinted at her. Surely she was joking. But she still wouldn't meet my eyes.

"Probably stolen."

"How could they have gotten your wallet?" I asked.

Juniper took a step back. "I just set it down for a minute or two. I was filming the party, and then Rachel fell into the water and you were rescuing her. I think I set my wallet down on your lifeguard chair."

"You *think?*"

My sister raised her chin, suddenly getting defensive. *"I know."*

How was this happening? Mom would already blame me for Juniper being at my college. What would happen when she found out Juniper's wallet was stolen? The party was full of people in masks and heavy makeup. Tonight the thief could literally be the devil.

Still, Juniper was a kid. What kind of things would she really be carrying in there? Sure, there'd be a driver's license, but was there anything else of value?

"What was in your wallet?" I asked. "Any credit cards?"

"Not credit cards," Juniper said. "But my license, debit card, and"—her voice began trembling—"two hundred dollars in cash."

"Two hundred!" People nearby were looking at us—so I'd probably yelled. I lowered my voice. "Why would you have that kind of money on you?"

Juniper flipped her hair back. "Well, I just got paid."

"Ever heard of a bank? It's a great place to store cash. Like—so it's safe from thieves."

"I..." Then Juniper's eyes began to water.

Ugh. She couldn't start crying.

"Sorry." I sighed and ran a hand through my wet hair.

Before my sister could reply, Rachel had walked up surrounded by her group of friends. She was still bedraggled in her flapper dress with all the fringe clumping weirdly together. "Excuse me, Holt?" She glanced apologetically at my sister. "Was my purse in the water?"

"No. Why?" I asked, though I was pretty sure it had something to do with Juniper's missing wallet.

She shook her head. "I just can't seem to find it."

"Okay. Do you think someone took it?"

Rachel's eyes widened, and she placed a hand on her heart. "Oh no. It can't be. That was a vintage coin purse that belonged to my grandma."

I frowned. So far Juniper was missing two hundred dollars, and Rachel was missing a family heirloom. Whenever Sean showed up, I needed to let him know he super-owed me.

"All right. Let's call campus police."

Fun fact: I've never called the police, but being the on-duty lifeguard somehow made me the most responsible college student at the college party.

So I made the call, doing my very best to act like I knew what I was doing.

Once I explained to the dispatcher about our purse snatcher, there was a long pause on the line. Finally, the dispatcher (who sounded younger than me) asked, "Do you know what day it is?"

Was that a trick question?

"Uh, October thirty-first."

"Correct," the voice said. "And do you know what *that* means?"

There was no way this was following police dispatcher protocol. Still, I answered the question. "It's Halloween."

"Ding, ding, ding," the guy said. "And do you know what *that* means?"

It meant I was done playing games. So I didn't answer. And I didn't answer very *loudly*.

The guy grumbled under his breath before saying, "It means campus cops are pretty busy with problems that rank a little higher than petty theft."

Petty theft?

"But"—heavy sigh—"we'll send someone over as soon as we can."

"When's that going to be?" I asked, but the line clicked off.

Juniper was waiting, snapping her fingers along with "The Addams Family." I was just trying to put on a brave face when my sister said, "Besides me and Rachel, seven other people are missing their wallets."

Please, no. Being a lifeguard is usually boring. You sit in a chair and watch people swim laps. I'd already saved someone's life, and now I was involved in a crime wave.

I closed my eyes and tightened my jaw. Until the police arrived—which would be a while—I was sort of in charge. The only other person paid to be at the Halloween bash was the snack supervisor, and no one was expecting her to step up.

"All right," I said loudly, then pulled Juniper close so only she could hear me. "Law enforcement is responding to calls they feel are a higher risk."

Juniper's eyes grew cartoonishly huge. "They're not coming?" she whispered.

"Not for a while," I said.

"But the thief might be getting away." Juniper stared at all the people in costumes.

"I know," I said, since that seemed better than informing my sister that the thief was probably long gone. It wasn't like hanging out at a party after you've robbed the place is a wise idea.

That's when I caught sight of a jacket that was half lab coat, half torn-up suit jacket. "Excuse me," I said to Juniper. Then I jogged toward Marcus—I know, I know, *no running by the pool.*

"Marcus!" I called.

When he heard me, Marcus stiffened, then hurried out a fire door. I followed because Marcus's sudden interest in *boring Halloween parties* made sense.

When I made it outside, I just caught a glimpse of Marcus turning around a corner of the building. He was walking so fast that I ran to catch up. "Marcus," I called when I was a little closer.

Could this be why he was at the party? Tell the story of the Drowned Girl, then get Rachel to create a distraction by falling into the pool, all so he could steal from unsuspecting students?

"Marcus!"

He finally stopped walking. "What?" he asked, sounding cranky.

Hold on. How was I supposed to ask a school acquaintance if he was a thief?

"People are missing personal property and"—*What was a good lie?*—"and no one's supposed to leave the pool." It sounded true. Should be true. But since the police weren't exactly excited to get here, who knew if they'd even investigate when they showed up.

"I can't stay." Marcus clutched his leather bag protectively, and the Dr. Jekyll side of his face tightened with fear.

"But you'll need to give a statement to the police."

Marcus took a step closer to the shadows—like he thought I wouldn't notice if he just disappeared. "Tell them I don't know anything."

I shook my head. "You know that won't work. Come back inside."

But Marcus didn't move.

"Fine. If you're so innocent, show me the bag."

Marcus took a step back. "No."

"Then come inside."

He hesitated, looking from his bag to the pool's entrance. Then he flinched as he saw something.

I heard Juniper before I saw her.

"You boys move fast," Juniper said—possibly a little winded.

"Yup," I said. Then, since I was currently in a stalemate, I said, "Juniper, this is Marcus; he's also studying to be an engineer."

My sister smiled. "Nice to officially meet you."

All Marcus did was grunt, and he was even tenser than before. Strange. Juniper typically had an unusual ability to get people to relax around her, but today she'd had the opposite effect.

"Come on," I said. "Let me take a look in the bag. Then I can tell the police I checked."

Marcus's jaw tightened, and while it was hard to tell from the dim glow of a distant streetlight, he may have blushed.

"Whatever," he finally said, and shoved the bag into my arms.

I opened the bag quickly so he wouldn't get a chance to change his mind.

"Oh…"

Granted, because he was willing to let me check implied the missing wallets weren't inside, but I still wasn't expecting a box of nice chocolates and a single rose.

"What is it?" Juniper asked, crowding into my space and trying to look inside.

"Umm." I closed the bag before Juniper could see. "It's not him. Let's go back. I'm freezing."

But I'd forgotten who my baby sister was. She snatched the bag from my hands and, in an instant, had it back open. "This is amazing!" Juniper said. "Who's the lucky lady?"

"I don't know," Marcus said.

Juniper and I looked at each other. Had we misheard?

He shook his head and muttered something under his breath. "I've been messaging someone since the start of the semester. We were going to introduce ourselves at the costume party. I'd go as Jekyll and Hyde, and she'd go as Zelda Fitzgerald."

Juniper gasped and said, "Oh no."

But I didn't get the problem until Marcus said, "I'd just spotted her when she fell into the pool."

So apparently Rachel wasn't dressed as any old flapper girl. She was specifically Zelda Fitzgerald.

"After Holt fished her out of the water and she'd talked to some friends, I went over to introduce myself. And…" From the way he was frowning down at the sidewalk, it made me wonder if Marcus was trying not to cry.

"And?" Juniper prompted.

"She told me she wasn't interested." Marcus cleared his throat. "So I left."

"You left? No!" Juniper's hands were firmly on her hips. "That can't be the end. You've been messaging each other for so long. There's no way she's *not* interested. Rachel must still be upset from falling into the water."

"Juniper, this is real life, not some princess movie." Both of my eyebrows were raised about as high as they could go. This is why little sisters don't belong on college campuses. But also, something about Marcus's story didn't make sense. "If you were here to meet a girl, why were you telling everyone about the Drowned Girl?"

"You know"—Marcus almost smirked—"it's Halloween. And it's fun."

"Who cares about that? This is about you and Rachel." Juniper shook her head. "I don't buy that she's not interested. Here." She took the chocolates out of the doctor's bag but left the rose. "Let me talk to her. Come back here in"—Juniper scrunched up her nose—"around forty minutes."

I raised an eyebrow. "That's a long time. What are you going to do, bake a cake?"

Juniper rolled her eyes. "Trust me. I know what I'm doing. Rachel almost drowned. That takes time to bounce back from."

"Look, I'll probably go find my buddies," Marcus said.

But my sister pointed a finger at his face. "Is this girl important to you?"

"Well...I..."

"That's what I thought," Juniper said. "See you soon." Then my sister took my arm and began dragging me back to the swimming pool.

"What about the cops?" Marcus asked.

"Don't worry about it," I called back.

It wasn't until we'd returned to the party that I realized I'd left my lifeguard post unmanned. Good thing nobody drowned.

I didn't know what Juniper's plan was regarding Marcus and Rachel's romance, and I was too scared to ask. While I walked straight to my lifeguard station, Juniper darted away once she spotted Rachel the Flapper Girl.

Without keeping a close eye on the clock, I'd guess Juniper talked to Flapper Girl for around five minutes. When my sister left, Rachel the Flapper Girl was shaking her head—but she'd kept the chocolates.

Before Juniper made it back to my lifeguard station, someone said, "Excuse me."

A female student stood in front of me with a pack of giggling friends. They hadn't even bothered with costumes. Instead, they all wore bikinis.

"Have you ever tried to rescue the Drowned Girl?"

"What? No." I shook my head. "It's pretend. That never happened."

"Oh." The ringleader took a step back. "Okay." And thankfully, they all left my station.

Juniper momentarily disappeared into the pack of students in swimsuits. She opened her mouth like she was about to comment on the Drowned Girl, but I'd heard enough of that story. So I said, "Whether or not Marcus and Rachel date is none of your business."

"Eh," Juniper said. "Sometimes love needs a little push. I'm here to help you, but that doesn't mean I can't help other people."

I grunted. Since when did I need Juniper's help?

"Don't act like you're fine," Juniper said. "You're clearly upset if you're working a party."

I frowned. "You know I'm a certified lifeguard, right?"

"And how many people are usually at the pool?"

My jaw ticked, but I tried to play it cool. "A few people swimming laps."

Juniper gestured to where a group of students was playing peek-aboo with jack-o'-lanterns. "So, it's safe to say this isn't a normal day in the office."

"So what? I'm covering half of someone else's shift because I'm nice." I tried to sound calm. "This isn't some act of desperation so awful that you had to lie to Mom and Dad to check on me."

Juniper's throat made a sound that was almost a laugh. "But you'd originally planned a date with your girlfriend."

"Well, sure, but no big plans."

"But there were plans?"

"Fine. Whatever." I sighed. "Tasha and I were going to watch *Jaws*."

"*Jaws?*" Juniper tilted her head like she was missing something.

"See," I said. "No big plans."

"That's not a Halloween movie," she said. "Why *Jaws*?"

"I don't know," I said. It was a mostly honest answer. I'm not a big *scary movie* guy. *Jaws* was at least suspenseful, and it was one of my dad's favorites.

"Holt?"

I shrugged. "Tasha's never seen it."

"I've never seen *Jaws*," Juniper said.

"What?" I shook my head. "No, Dad had us watch it. Like it was maybe a Saturday afternoon when Casey didn't have sports."

"Yeah," Juniper said. "Dad showed you and Casey while I was out on a bonding session with Mom."

"Well, then tell Dad you want to see it," I said. "He'd watch it with you."

Before Juniper could further pry into my business, a shout caught our attention. Was I about to do another underwater rescue?

"Here!" a man in an alligator costume called. He was at the opposite side of the deep end, pointing down at the water. Or I assume it was the water. There was quite a lot of dry ice misting over that area, so I mostly saw the green alligator swirling through the fog.

What now?

Please don't make me get back in the water. I'd just gotten relatively dry. There hadn't been a splash, and there wasn't a dark form of a person underwater.

I strode through the crowd to get to the Alligator Man with Juniper following in my wake. Once I was standing right next to the guy, I could clearly see a collection of purses and wallets at the bottom of the swimming pool.

It felt like overkill when Juniper grabbed my biceps and announced, "There's my wallet."

This was getting interesting. If I had to guess, the thief had removed all the cash and then dumped the purses into the water so they wouldn't be caught with the evidence. I'd need to get back in the pool, but at least it had nothing to do with the Drowned Girl.

"Any idea when this happened?" I asked Alligator Man.

He shook his head. "I just noticed them."

"Juniper, take some photos of that," I said as I went to the back wall to open one of the pool crates. I emptied an assortment of balls from a mesh bag and then returned to the side of the pool with the empty bag.

Maybe I should wait for the police to come, but who knew what time that would be, and I needed to confirm my hunch that just the cash was removed. I handed Juniper my sweatshirt and towel, then dove into the water.

So much for staying dry.

I swam to the bottom of the pool and grabbed an assortment of wallets and purses, putting them into the mesh bag. There were two or three left when my lungs began throbbing and my vision began to speckle. I pushed off the bottom and quickly had my head above the surface.

Juniper was waiting. "You told Mom college was boring. This seems pretty exciting."

I didn't bother to answer before I swam back down to retrieve the remaining wallets. Once I had them all, I shot up again and swam to the side before pulling myself out of the water.

People—mostly the victims of the thefts—were crowding around me as I sat there dripping, with my legs dangling into the water.

"The purple one's mine," a woman said.

People kept getting closer and closer, until there were sickening tingles on my neck like spiders were crawling up my spine. My personal space bubble was getting invaded, and I was having trouble focusing. It was Juniper's "Stay back" that checked everyone's movements. The tingling down my neck began to dissipate, and I could breathe again. Juniper handed over my towel and waited until I'd pulled on the Baywatch sweatshirt to ask, "What's the plan?"

"Which one's yours?" I asked.

"There." She pointed to the bag. "With the Eiffel Tower on it."

The thing Juniper called a wallet wasn't something that would fit in a pants pocket. It might be classified as a *clutch*, but it definitely wasn't a wallet.

Picking up my sister's clutch, I ignored the groans and muttered comments of people thinking I was giving my sister preferential treatment.

"Check it," I said. "Are you missing anything besides the cash?"

Juniper opened the clutch, and her eyes got big as she riffled through the contents. "It's not," she said.

"Not what?"

"Not missing. All of my cash is still here."

"Are you sure?" I paused mid-toweling my dripping hair to look at her.

Juniper rolled her eyes but removed a clump of wet cash that was all stuck together and began the slow process of peeling the bills apart as she counted. "Two hundred," she finally said.

"Anything else missing?"

She shook her head.

I squeezed my eyes shut. This wasn't making sense. First someone had taken the risk of stealing nine people's wallets, and then, instead of keeping them, they all got dumped in the pool.

"Come on, man, give us our stuff," said one of the hockey players.

"Hold on," I said. I picked a random one out of the mesh bag. Pulling out the license, I read the name. "Chance Rivers?"

"Here." A guy stepped forward dressed like some cartoon character holding a half-eaten caramel apple.

"Check if anything's missing," I said.

The guy nodded before looking through his wallet. "Nope," he said. "It's all here."

"Thanks," I said. Next, I picked up a sequined purse and checked the license. "Emily Harris?"

The process repeated until the bag was empty, and only Flapper Girl was waiting.

Nothing had been missing. Granted, a few people weren't sure of the exact amount of cash they'd been carrying, and it was hard counting bills that were all stuck together. But as far as they could tell, it was all accounted for.

"Isn't there one more?" Rachel asked—though she could see as easily as I could that the bag was empty.

"Sorry," I said.

Rachel raised her hand to her forehead. "I promised Mom I would take good care of Grandma's coin purse. And now"—her voice broke—"now I lost it at a college party."

Something in my chest (possibly my heart) loosened. And yet part of me, the cynical, just-got-dumped-with-no-warning part, wasn't buying the performance.

I glanced at my sister since she's better at judging body language. But Juniper wasn't looking at Flapper Girl. She had her nose scrunched and was frowning at the diving blocks.

"What's that?" she asked.

My vision was a little off from the chlorine, but I got up and walked to the closest diving block.

"Do you see it?" she asked.

While standing, all I saw were the cobwebs stretched across the metal frame. However, once I squatted, I spotted the beaded coin purse.

"Got it," I said aloud, but internally I wondered what the odds were that the heirloom coin purse was safe on dry land when everyone else's wallets were dumped in the water.

Rachel and Juniper were immediately crowding around me. I handed Rachel the coin purse, but she didn't open it. Instead, she held it tight to her chest like it might disappear.

"Are you missing anything?" Juniper asked.

Flapper Girl shook her head. "It doesn't matter. I have Grandma's purse. We don't know how much time she has left. I couldn't lose this part of her." She took a few more moments holding it close before undoing the snap and looking inside. "It's all here."

"You're sure?" I asked, trying to get a look inside.

Rachel the Flapper Girl clipped the bag shut. "Positive."

"Great," I said.

Around me, the other theft victims stood waiting. "Will we need to talk to the police?" Hockey Player asked.

Cartoon Character shrugged. "Nothing's missing. Can't we forget about it?"

"Let's get back to the party," said a sparkly mermaid.

It seemed like everyone—including Juniper—was nodding.

Seriously? Someone had gone around stealing from nine different people, and they all wanted to forget about it since they got their stuff back?

Shouldn't the original theft be looked into?

"I'll call the police and tell them they don't need to bother coming out," Hockey Player announced.

"Wonderful," Rachel the Flapper Girl whispered beside me.

I stared at her. She seemed relieved, but how could Rachel be involved? Juniper's clutch was taken sometime between Rachel falling into the water and Rachel regaining consciousness.

But had Rachel really been unconscious? When I'd checked, she hadn't been breathing, but there'd been a pulse...

It was possible to stop breathing but have a pulse. Still, had she really coughed up the water, or had Rachel been holding water in her mouth and spat it out at the right moment for a miraculous recovery?

"You look pretty serious for a guy who's saved the day twice."

I frowned at Juniper. "You're fine with this?"

She shrugged. "With what?"

"With the thief getting away with robbery."

"They didn't actually take anything, so what's the big deal?"

"What's the big deal?" I raised my eyebrows, then muttered, "You can be such a kid sometimes."

I started walking back to my lifeguard station, but from Juniper's "Hey!" I knew I was in trouble.

"Do you think the police will care?" Juniper began marching toward me. "They're too busy to bother showing up when the wallets were missing. How much do you think they'll investigate when we tell them everything was returned?" Juniper had reached me and jabbed my chest with her index finger.

I glared at her. Sure, Juniper had a point, but letting the thief off the hook was wrong.

When I didn't answer, Juniper rolled her eyes. "Do you plan on solving this?"

A lock of wet hair fell onto my face, and I brushed it back. "I'd like to know what happened."

"Here," Juniper said. "I set my wallet down when I started filming." Before I could tell my sister that filming a college pool party was inappropriate, she was shoving her phone in my face.

Huh. There was Rachel's peacock feather bobbing around behind a crowd of people. It seemed like she was talking to someone. I moved to get to the same perspective that Juniper had when she'd recorded.

The snack station was set up by that wall. "Look," I said, showing Juniper the video. "Do you think the snack person saw who Rachel was talking to?"

"It's worth asking," Juniper said and began walking to the food table without waiting to see if I followed.

Of course I followed. Not only did I want to solve this, but Mom would kill me if I let Juniper out of my sight at a college party. My sister's purposeful stride cleared a path, and I moved in her shadow. When she reached the snack table, Juniper tossed her hair back and smiled.

"Punch or candy apples?" the server asked. Up close, I could see her vampire costume was definitely an homage to Dracula.

Something mischievous sparkled in Juniper's eyes, and I said, "Information," before my sister got any wild ideas.

Female Dracula eyed me warily. "I don't know anything. I've been here all night."

"Of course, you've been busy," Juniper was quick to say. "But isn't part of your job overhearing secrets?" Then Juniper winked like they were sharing an inside joke.

Female Dracula frowned at Juniper. Then she opened her mouth and shut it again like she couldn't figure out what to do with my sister. Finally, Female Dracula sighed. "What do you want to know?"

Juniper took out her phone and showed a frozen image of Flapper Girl's peacock feather close to the bar. "The woman who fell in the pool was by your table before her accident. Did you notice who she talked to?"

"No." Female Dracula had a stubborn set to her jaw. "Like I said, I don't know anything. I've been minding my own business, working the snack station all night."

"*All* night?" Juniper asked.

"Yes, *all* night." Female Dracula sighed extra loudly. "Look, I'm getting paid minimum wage to make sure no one spikes the punch."

"What if you needed to...?" My sister nodded toward the restrooms.

"I wait." Female Dracula tore open a bag of candy corn and added it to an almost empty bowl. "Ask the lifeguard. Some jobs you can't leave."

"You're so right." Juniper smiled widely and took a new cup of punch. "Thanks for talking with us."

Once we were back at my lifeguard station, I asked Juniper, "Did you film anything else?"

"Well..." She bit her lip. "Don't be mad, but I kind of filmed your rescue."

She did what?

"That's really creepy," I said. "What if Rachel died?"

"I don't know." Juniper gave a half shrug. "At least there'd be proof you did everything to save her."

Awkward pause. Then Juniper asked, "Do you want to watch?"

I nodded since I couldn't quite say the words out loud.

Juniper balanced her phone on the top of her punch cup and started a new video. It began right after I'd jumped into the water. There I was, swimming toward Rachel the Flapper Girl, with a crowd of people watching from the pool's edge. Then blobs of movement as I got to Rachel and then we finally broke the water's surface—timed perfectly to "Ghostbusters" playing in the background.

At the point where I shook the hair out of my face, someone whistled. How had I missed that?

Then came the hockey guys helping lift Rachel out. It was all how I remembered it. But when she was being lifted from the pool, the camera caught the slightest contraction of Flapper Girl's body, almost like...she was breathing.

"Why did she fall?" I asked Juniper.

"Uhhh..." Juniper's eyes were wide, and she seemed extra young. "She said she tripped out of her shoe."

I shook my head. "But did you see it happen?"

"Not actually." Juniper scrunched her nose.

Without asking, I took the phone and began swiping through the video. For once Juniper didn't argue but hovered beside me, watching the screen. I paused the image on the best shot of the solitary shoe by the pool's edge.

What were the chances? Flapper Girl had one shoe on the cement, the other at the bottom of the pool.

It was chaotic.

A little too chaotic, like the whole thing was staged.

But Rachel the Flapper Girl couldn't have stolen the wallets since Juniper's went missing during the time of the drowning scare. While I was muddling through the timeline, Juniper took a drink. "This tastes funny," she said, frowning down at her punch.

What?

Please, no.

I grabbed the cup and gave it a good sniff. It had an almost bitter scent. Even before I tasted the punch, I knew it was spiked with whiskey.

"She had one job," I muttered, looking from the cup to Female Dracula's snack station. "When you gave me punch earlier, it tasted normal, and that was right before Flapper Gir—or Rachel fell into the pool."

"Yeah," Juniper said. "So Lindsey did leave her station."

"Who's Lindsey?"

"Her." Juniper nodded toward Female Dracula.

"Right," I said, but how did Juniper know her name? I didn't remember hearing it. "Come on," I said. "I know who Rachel was talking to by the snack station."

This time I led the march.

Just like with Marcus, I was in a tough spot. Outright accusing someone of theft is kind of awkward...or taboo. Maybe both.

But there must've been something in my stride or the set of my jaw because Female Dracula's face fell, and she held up her hands. "I didn't keep any of it."

What? Had she just confessed? I glanced at Juniper. Was being a detective usually this easy?

"So you're admitting to stealing—"

Before I could finish the sentence, Female Dracula was interrupting. "Yup, I did it. I stole everything."

Okay, this was going way smoother than I'd expected.

"And your accomplice?" I asked.

Female Dracula's shoulders tensed. "I did it all by myself."

"But what about...?" I tilted my head toward the pool.

Female Dracula shrugged. "I saw an opportunity."

My eyes met Juniper's. Neither of us was buying this performance. Juniper popped her hip, and it was like a warrior preparing for battle. But a new voice cut in before Juniper could speak.

"It's not her fault."

Juniper and I turned to find Flapper Girl standing there. Rachel had cleaned up the streaky makeup, but the wet tassels on her dress still left her looking bedraggled.

"It's because of me. I needed money to get a bus ticket. Lindsey just wanted to help." Rachel moved to stand in front of the snack table like she was guarding her friend.

"Help by stealing from nine people?" I asked.

"Rachel had nothing to do with the theft," Lindsey said, moving to the front of the snack station. "Some guy was talking about the Drowned Girl, and I asked Rachel to do a reenactment."

"I knew the pool accident was staged," I said to Juniper—though I'm sure the other two heard.

Juniper crossed her arms, and Lindsey and Rachel were met with the full force of teenage anger. "What reason could you possibly have that would make theft the best solution?"

Rachel blinked rapidly as she tried to hide her watering eyes. Unlike before, this distress seemed genuine. "My parents don't have a lot of money. And they think Grandma will hang on for a while more. But"—a solitary tear slid down her cheek—"I just know I have to see her now."

"Oh no!" Juniper's eyes were round.

I shook my head. The story about the sick Grandmother was probably true. Still, Rachel could be a con artist who knew how to lie.

"How much money do you need?" Juniper asked.

I stared at my sister. How naive was she? "Don't give them any money," I said. "They've already stolen from you."

"But they gave the money back," Juniper argued.

"He's right." Rachel shook her head. "I couldn't take your money."

Seriously? Rachel had already been a part of a scheme to take Juniper's money. I coughed pointedly, and Rachel's face reddened. But apparently her friend had enough of my attitude because Female Dracula raised her chin—this was extra dramatic thanks to the vampire's teeth—and said, "All Rachel wants is to see her grandma. She had no idea what I was doing."

"Rachel just pretended to drown because you asked her to?" My voice was extra skeptical.

Female Dracula's shrug was extra pronounced due to the cape. "It's Halloween. I dared her to. It would've been fine if I hadn't accidentally taken Rachel's beaded purse. I didn't know it was hers or that it had sentimental value. When I found out, I had to tell Rachel her purse was safe, and then..."

"I asked her to return everything," Rachel finished. "She hadn't even taken the money out of the wallets. I thought if everyone got their stuff back, it would be okay."

"You'll tell the police what happened?" Female Dracula asked, staring sadly at the ground.

Right. The police. A crime had been committed, and the courts should be involved.

"Well..." I hesitated. It wasn't like I enjoyed being the person in charge, but could I really let a thief get away? No matter how *good* the reason, a crime had been committed.

"Please, Holt." Juniper tugged childishly at my arm.

"Monster Mash" was playing in the background. And the way the three of them looked at me made me feel like I was the monster.

But I wasn't the monster because I wasn't the thief.

My sister unleashed her doe eyes. "Rachel just wants to see her family."

"Juniper, just because they got caught this time doesn't mean they won't try it again."

"Fine." Female Dracula crossed her arms. "I'll make a full confession. Rachel had nothing to do with this." Lindsey stepped toward Rachel, her cape fluttering as she moved. "Sorry I couldn't help you get to Canterway."

Both Juniper and I stiffened. But I was the one who asked, "Your grandma lives in Canterway?"

Rachel nodded—it seemed like if she tried to speak, she'd start crying.

"Why does it matter?" Lindsey asked.

"Canterway's on my way home," Juniper said. "I can drive her."

"Once you clear it with Mom," I said—no way was I letting my sister spend hours alone with a thieving stranger without parental permission.

"But what about...?" Rachel nodded toward me.

Did I really have to call the police? Maybe I wasn't a monster, just a villain in a kid's movie. If I wasn't careful, I'd start smashing pumpkins in front of the agriculture building.

A man's voice cut into my thoughts. "Sorry, I'm late. How'd it go?"

It was Sean.

Sean was here. And in charge. I was no longer the lifeguard on duty.

"It went how you'd expect." I shrugged. "Some wallets were stolen, and they turned up in the swimming pool."

"Dumb prank." Sean shook his head. "I hate Halloween."

I peeled off the Baywatch sweatshirt and handed it to him. Sean took the sweatshirt but frowned when he found it was damp. "What'd you do? Jump into the pool with this on?"

"Sure. Let's go with that."

When I didn't give more details, Sean said, "Well, thanks for helping out," and walked away.

Which meant...

"My shift's over," I said to Juniper. "I'm gonna put on some dry clothes, and then we can head to my apartment. You're not driving home tonight."

"And the—" Rachel weakly raised her grandma's coin purse like that would summon the cops.

"None of my property was stolen. None of the victims want to press charges. And I'm off duty." I shrugged. "Do whatever you'd like."

"Holt!" Juniper vaulted into me for an attack hug. "You do have a heart."

"Sure," I said. Thoughts of my ex tried to force their way into my brain, but I managed to shove them back down. "Get Rachel's number. If Mom says it's okay, you can drop her off in Canterway tomorrow."

"Great." Juniper already had her phone's contacts page open.

Since I didn't like leaving Juniper alone, I changed as fast as humanly possible. But while I was gone, Marcus had returned, and he was talking to Rachel the Flapper Girl. She was blushing and holding the rose while Juniper watched like a teenage fairy godmother.

Another happy ending.

I was startled when a woman said, "Your lifeguarding skills are really impressive." She was dressed as a butterfly—or maybe a fairy.

"Thanks," I said.

"Here." Her eyelids fluttered as she held out a cup with a phone number Sharpied along the side. "Call me sometime."

I took a step back and, on instinct, said, "Thanks, but I have a girlfriend."

Butterfly Woman shook her head with a self-deprecating laugh. "Of course you do. Tell her she's lucky."

Then Butterfly Woman left, but her final comment stung. Tasha found being my girlfriend so amazing that she'd dumped me and left me alone for Halloween.

I turned around, and Juniper was there staring at me. Her eyes were watery, and immediately I began scanning the room for which creepy college guy I needed to have a talk with.

"Can we go now?" Juniper asked in a quiet voice.

"Yeah," I said. "Let's get out of here." Again I looked around, trying to find the guy who'd upset my baby sister.

"Relax," she said. "I'm fine."

I didn't quite believe her. "What is it?" I asked. "What happened?"

Juniper sniffled. "Let's just go."

"Hey," I said. "If there's someone I need to talk to…"

Juniper rolled her eyes. "Would you relax on the big-brother routine? I'm fine."

But I stood there waiting.

Juniper scrunched up her nose. "You know I can just drive home."

"All right," I said. "Go home." But I was pretty sure Juniper wouldn't be able to leave without sharing at least one pint of ice cream with me post-breakup.

Juniper stared at me, but instead of the usual fight in her eyes, she just looked—defeated. "Fine," she said. "First, a group of college girls dressed like swimsuit models paraded themselves in front of you and you didn't even notice."

I raised an eyebrow at Juniper. No way that was true. Not that I can't get a date, but women don't throw themselves at me.

"Come on," Juniper said. "Those girls in bathing suits asking the Drowned Girl just wanted an excuse to talk to the heroic lifeguard. And then, when you told that butterfly woman you had a girlfriend...I don't know...It was like you'd forgotten you were single, and when you remembered, you just looked—sad."

Sad?

Was I sad?

I ran a hand through my damp hair. "Yeah, well, I wasn't expecting the breakup." I took a deep breath. "I guess it'll take some time to adjust."

Juniper let out a little whimper and threw her arms around me. Honestly, you'd think I'd just admitted to crying myself to sleep at night—which I don't do.

"Okay," I said once the hug had gone on long enough. "Juniper? Come on." I shifted out of her grasp. "Let's go to my apartment."

"But we're having a moment." Juniper pouted.

"But there's ice cream at my apartment."

My sister perked up. "Promise?"

"Yeah, I promise." I slung an arm casually over Juniper's shoulder as we walked to the exit. "And if you want, we can even watch *Jaws.*"

"*Jaws?*" Juniper wrinkled her nose. "Has anyone ever told you that's not a Halloween movie?"

I rolled my eyes. "Just you."

"Holt?" Juniper asked as we stepped into the night.

"Yeah?"

Her eyes sparkled in the darkness. "Now that you've solved the Flapper Girl Mystery, you can solve the Mystery of the Drowned Girl."

I groaned. "You know that's just a ghost story."

Juniper giggled. "Happy Halloween."

Lily Stirling

Holt Jacobs and his sister Juniper return years later for *A Not So Shocking Murde*r. With no coffee and a dead guy, it promises to be one killer vacation. To learn more,

visit *lilystirling.com*.

Chapter Six

Harry's Haunted Halloween

Victoria L.K. Williams

The oversized gray cat. No, let's be honest. The fat gray cat nudged his head against the teenager's chin and then swatted at a tendril of bright pink hair that was falling out of her messy bun.

"Harry, stop! I can't see through you. Move!" The young girl leaned to the side and tried to look at the photo album on the table around the cat, but Harry wasn't in the mood to be ignored. He moved, only not the way Kelly Sky had wanted. Instead of getting down and letting her have the space to look at the photo album, he turned his back to her, stepped over to the middle of the photo album, and plopped himself down.

"Oh Harry, you're impossible." Kelly gave a laugh and tried to push the cat out of the way, but Harry just settled down more firmly and turned to stare at her in defiance.

In the short time that Kelly had been living at the Azalea Plantation, she knew that stare very well. Harry was going to have his way. There was never any doubt about this. Kelly reached into her jeans and pulled out a few morsels of kitty treats. She'd learned to always keep them on her to win over Harry, who ruled the roost at the plantation. Smiling at his grateful purr, Kelly couldn't help how lucky she felt. After 16 years of being an orphan, she finally felt like she had a home. And that was all because of Lizzie Higgins, the owner of Azalea Plantation, who had taken her in after their mutual involvement with Kelly's employer's murder and made her feel welcomed and loved.

"And that's why that cat is so darn fat. Just pick him up and move him, Kelly."

Kelly jumped, feeling guilty about being caught, and looked behind her. Nora Meadows stood in the doorway with her hand on one hip and shaking her fingers at Kelly with her other hand, but still smiling. Nora was the manager of the bed-and-breakfast and more family than an employee.

"I don't give these to him that often," Kelly protested as she held the treats close enough for Harry to sniff and grab his attention. Then she moved her hand away from the photo album and placed the morsels on the floor next to her. Harry didn't miss the opportunity and jumped down from the photo album to get his treat.

"What are you looking at, Kelly?" Nora asked as she walked over to Kelly and leaned over her shoulder.

"I found these on the bookshelf. They're ancient. Can you believe the costumes these women wore?" Nora looked down at the pictures and smiled. She had spent many hours with Lizzie

Higgins, the current owner of Azalea Plantation, doing this same thing.

"Oh, you have a Halloween album. The Higgins family threw some fantastic Halloween parties, and costumes were mandatory. The one you're looking at had a 1900s theme, celebrating when Elizabeth Higgins took over the plantation and turned it around. She was one of the first women to run a plantation on her own and do it successfully without the use of slaves."

"Every time I hear about Elizabeth Higgins, I'm in awe. She must have been a fascinating woman. I can't imagine running a large plantation and all the intricate working facilities that go with it. And raise a family on her own in addition."

"She was most certainly an amazing woman, and our Lizzie is much like her. Elizabeth was the first of her family to add flower gardens as part of the commerce of the plantation, just like the cattle and food crops. In her time, flowers were a luxury for the most affluent families to enjoy."

Kelly listened to Nora's history lesson and turned the page of the album. As she did, an elegant parchment invitation fell to the ground. Kelly picked it up, staring at the elaborate handwriting.

"Look, this is the invitation to the party. Nora, we were looking for something to do for Halloween at the plantation's bed-and-breakfast party. Why not reenact this? I know it's short notice, but I think we could pull it off. Wouldn't that be fun?" Nora took the invitation from Kelly's hand and gave it a puzzled look.

"I don't remember ever seeing this invitation before. But you're right, it's exactly what we were looking for and with all the renovations on the old homestead, it's perfect. I'm sure Lizzie will agree to this."

The two women grinned at each other, knowing even if Lizzie didn't agree at first, they could convince her it was an idea and to move forward. Nora reached into her apron pocket and pulled out her notebook to write down their ideas. The two women spent the next twenty minutes talking over their thoughts on how to create a successful Halloween party with a turn-of-the-century theme. They agreed Kelly would get on the computer right away and create the invitations so they could get out in the afternoon's mail. There was no time to lose. Halloween was only a couple of weeks away. As they sat there, Kelly on the floor petting Harry, and Nora sitting in the rocking chair next to her, they didn't notice the woman standing in the doorway watching them.

"From the sounds of your plans, you two might need some extra help. What can I do?"

The woman who had been watching Nora and Kelly walked into the room and both women looked up and grinned at Lizzie Higgins, the current owner of Azalea plantation, and Kelly's Guardian.

Kelly jumped to her feet, almost tripping over Harry, who hadn't budged, hoping for more treats.

"Look at this fantastic invitation we found. We're thinking about re-creating the party for Halloween. What do you think?" Kelly asked, handing Lizzie the parchment invitation.

"With Nora's knack for organizing a party, you won't have any problems pulling this off. And I think I have just what you need. Nora, do you remember all those boxes we found in the attic? I'm sure I saw costumes and decorations that will be perfect for our party." Lizzie handed the invitation back to Kelly, giving her approval without hesitation.

Nora nodded her agreement with Lizzie and then turned her attention to Kelly, giving her the instructions. "You're right. There are plenty of things up in the attic that will be perfect for the party. Kelly, why don't you go up and explore? I want to go over a few items on this list I wrote with Lizzie, and then we can meet you there. Most of what you'll want are in the back west corner."

Kelly hugged each of the women tightly before she turned and ran from the room, heading to the second floor and the entrance to the attic. Harry was hot on her heels, not wanting to miss a thing.

It didn't take long for Kelly to find the items in the west corner of the attic, and she happily began opening trunks and digging into boxes. She was so involved with her search that she missed two important things.

The first was the scattering of azalea blossoms that were out of season, but Harry knew what they meant, and he went over and meowed as he sniffed the blossoms. Lizzie and Harry had both learned that the blossoms indicated the spirit of Elizabeth Higgins was nearby. She had either been or was coming. Hearing Harry's meow, Kelly looked around her. She, too, knew what the azaleas symbolized, although she'd only seen them a few times herself.

This time the beautiful, shimmering form of Elizabeth Higgins wasted no time appearing. The specter rarely spoke, giving her messages with hints and writings in the dust. Kelly gave a tentative wave to Elizabeth, but she had no fear of the ghost. More than once, Elizabeth Higgins had come to the help of either Kelly or Lizzie. Turning back to the trunk she was sitting in front of, Kelly reached in and pulled out a beautiful gown. Standing up, she held it up in front of her and looked at Elizabeth for approval. The ghostly figure smiled and gave a nod, and Kelly knew this was the costume she'd wear for the party. She watched as Elizabeth floated amongst the memorabilia from the past, reaching her hand out to touch things that made her smile.

The second thing that Kelly failed to notice was the creaking of the stairs as heavy footsteps climbed up into the attic.

"What are you doing up here? You have no business going through our family things."

The angry male voice startled Kelly enough that she dropped the dress from her hands and turned to find Freddie Higgins staring at her, his hands on his hips and a sneer crossed his lips.

"I have permission to be up here, Freddie. Does Lizzie know you're here?"

"I don't need my cousin's permission to walk around my family home. But what are you doing, and why are you snooping?"

Freddie took a threatening step toward Kelly, and she cringed, sidestepping him. Elizabeth had disappeared at the sound of Freddie's voice, but now Lizzie saw her out of the corner of her eye coming up behind Freddie.

Without warning, Elizabeth reached out and gave a gentle push to a pile of hat boxes that were stacked to the side of Freddie. The boxes came down with a crash and Freddie whirled around, wondering what was going on. But as he looked around, there was nothing to be seen. This wasn't the first time Elizabeth Higgins had pulled a prank on Freddie, and it was usually when she was defending Lizzie or Kelly.

The sound of the falling boxes brought Lizzie to the top of the stairs, and she quickly took in the situation. She wasn't at all pleased to find Freddie in her home and realized he was trying to intimidate Kelly.

"What are you doing up here, Freddie? Why are you wandering around the house without letting us know you're here? You don't live here, and you're not a paying guest at the Bed-and-Breakfast, so I would appreciate it if you had the courtesy to knock on the front door and let us know you're here."

While Freddie stuttered his answer, Lizzie looked around, taking in the situation. Kelly was fine and when Lizzie caught sight of the azalea blossoms and the fallen boxes, it took little for her to put two and two together and she tried to hide her grin.

"Enough Freddie. Please go downstairs. I'm sure Nora can provide you with a cup of coffee. Kelly and I have things to do up here. I'll talk to you later."

Dismissing Freddie without a backward glance, Lizzie stepped over to Kelly and admired the dress she was holding. Her cousin had little choice but to turn and go back down the stairs. This was a scene often played out between the cousins; Freddie trying to assert his claim on the family plantation that he had no right to—and that angered him. Now that Kelly was part of the household, his resentment now had included her as well. The two women held their breath, hoping their spectral ancestor would not trip him as he rushed toward the kitchen. Freddie hurried down the stairs, upset not by Lizzie's words but by, once again, something spooky happening on the plantation.

Lizzie added her approval to the dress that Kelly had picked out and pointed out a few other items the younger girl had missed that would be perfect for the party. Kelly beamed at Lizzie's suggestions, feeling a renewed sense of excitement for the upcoming event.

"Well, I'd better go downstairs and smooth Freddie's feathers. Come down when you're done, but don't carry too many things. Just stack what you want in a corner, and we'll have somebody bring them down for you." Lizzie said, her voice tinged with the patience of someone accustomed to managing family squabbles.

Lizzie gave Kelly a quick hug and then, with a sigh, headed downstairs. She looked back to see if Harry was going to follow her, but he had his nose deep in another open box. Shrugging, Lizzie headed down to confront her cousin.

"I don't know what Freddie has against me, Harry. But I sure don't like being alone with him," Kelly confided to the cat, who looked up at her with cobwebs dangling from his whiskers.

Kelly reached out to the pile and grabbed a small box that was sitting inside the trunk. Opening it up, she found some photos and recognized Elizabeth. At the bottom of the pile of photos was a small wooden container. Opening it, she found a beautiful gold brooch with a small clasp where something had once been attached. Digging through the box, she tried to find the charm that must've been part of the brooch. But the box was empty except for more pictures. She scrutinized the pictures with care, noting that most of them showed Elizabeth wearing the brooch. Squinting her eyes, she made out the shape of a heart that had been attached to the piece of jewelry and was now missing.

"That's a shame. I wonder where it disappeared to?" Kelly asked Harry. But Harry wasn't the one that answered. Elizabeth's form shimmered and stood in front of Kelly, pointing to her brooch. She made the shape of a heart with her fingertips in the air, and Kelly knew she was right. The locket had been heart-shaped and attached to the brooch.

Just as quickly as she had appeared, Elizabeth disappeared, but she left a message in the attic's dust that gave a single direction: Find.

Kelly loved a challenge, and she quickly began searching through the boxes and trunks, hoping to find the missing locket. She moved from one corner of the attic to the next, her movements becoming more frantic as each box revealed only more dust and cobwebs. She found old letters, faded ribbons, and even a cracked mirror, but no locket.

Then she glanced toward an old stand-up mirror that stood in the corner. She couldn't help but laugh at herself; her pink hair had cobwebs stuck to it, and her nose was dirty from the dust. Sitting back on one of the closed trunks, Kelly looked around the attic, wondering where to search next. The silence of the attic seemed to mock her determination.

But before she could start in another section of the attic, she heard Nora calling from downstairs, announcing that lunch was ready.

"Coming," she called back and then looked around the attic one more time, hoped Elizabeth might reappear, but the room was empty. "I'll keep looking, Elizabeth, and if I can, I'll find your locket," Kelly whispered into the air. Only silence answered her, but as she walked toward the stairs to leave the attic, she found another cluster of azalea blossoms and knew Elizabeth had heard.

Kelly entered the kitchen, where the warm smell of homemade bread and Nora's famous chicken soup greeted her. Lizzie sat at the table, waiting for her.

"Find anything interesting up there?" Lizzie asked, her eyes twinkling with curiosity.

"Actually, I did. Look at this brooch and these pictures. Along with a few more cobwebs for my collection," Kelly replied with a grin. She promptly filled Lizzie and Nora in on her encounter with Elizabeth and the discovery of the brooch and the missing heart-shaped charm.

"I must find it. I sort of promised," Kelly said, her determination clear. "After lunch, I think we should go through the old family records. There might be something about Elizabeth's locket."

Lizzie nodded. "Agreed. Maybe there's a diary or a letter that mentions the locket."

Nora set a steaming bowl of soup in front of Kelly and patted her shoulder. "We'll figure it out, dear. Elizabeth is guiding you for a reason. There's a connection waiting to be uncovered."

Kelly took a sip of the soup, feeling a warmth spread through her that was more than just the food. It was the sense of family, of belonging, and the excitement of the mystery that lay ahead.

As they finished their lunch and made their plans for the afternoon, Kelly felt a renewed sense of purpose. She glanced at the cluster of azalea blossoms she had placed on the table, a silent reminder of the ghostly guidance she had received. They would solve this mystery together.

Kelly and Nora lost no time with the party planning, and they roped in everyone they could to help. This included Lizzie and her greenhouse and garden staff. Some workers who were adding a winter garden house to the massive gardens on the estate were coaxed into helping. But in the back of Kelly's mind was the missing locket and her promise to Elizabeth.

Nora took charge of the refreshments for the party, while Kelly got to work on sending out personalized invitations. The neighbors, staff, and old friends knew there was always a Halloween open house at Azalea Plantation, but Kelly wanted to be sure they knew to come in costume. She lost no time creating an almost perfect replica of the invitation she had found for the original party.

Azalea Plantation had been converted to a bed-and-breakfast years ago, and at the party, guests would wander into the main house and out into the exquisite gardens the Higgins family was famous for. The only place that would be off limits was Lizzie's home, which was the original plantation house, and the private pond and gardens around her residence. But that still left plenty of areas for the guests to gather and for Kelly to plan decorations for.

Thankfully, Nora and Lizzie decorated the grounds and house for the guests to enjoy for fall, so all Kelly would need to add is the Halloween touches and bring in the period's elegance. That would be easy with a small band, costumes, and flowers from the greenhouses. On the morning of the party, there would be a children's event for pumpkin carving, and the staff would join in to help the kids and demonstrate their skills in carving. There would be plenty of pumpkins to use for the party.

The invitations had been hand-delivered or sent via email, and already the responses were flooding in. Lizzie and Nora were handling the accommodations for out-of-town guests, and Kelly had created an oversized spreadsheet that hung on the kitchen bulletin board to keep track of the guests. So far, there had been few refusals and from the phone calls that were coming in, everyone in town seemed excited about the twist on the traditional party.

It was already a week before the big event. Where had the past week gone? Nora had sent Kelly down to the greenhouse with a list of herbs she needed, and Lizzie had disappeared into town on an errand.

"Looks like it's you and me, Harry. Come on, let's take the long way to the greenhouse and let you get in some exercise."

Kelly paused at the kitchen door after checking the bulletin board and snapped her fingers to get Harry's attention. The cat was curled up on the window seat and showed no interest in Kelly's suggestion. "Oh, come on Harry, don't be so lazy!" Without giving the cat a moment to figure out what she was up to, Kelly scooped the cat up and walked out the door. When he squirmed to get into a more comfortable position, Kelly laughed and put him on the ground, telling Harry he was going to have to walk. Harry seemed to pout, but when Kelly started walking down the path to the greenhouse, he swished his tail and hurried to catch up to her, not wanting to miss a thing.

It was a beautiful day, still hot, but the evenings promised cooler weather, and Emma took her time, wanting to enjoy the gardens. She was also hoping that Elizabeth would reappear and give her some direction on searching for the locket, but Azalea Plantation's resident ghost did not make an appearance. Kelly gathered the herbs on Nora's list, picked a handful of seasonal flowers for her bedroom, and headed back to the bed-and-breakfast. As she got closer, she noticed Lizzie's car was back, and she smiled to herself. Then she broke out into a wide grin when she saw a young woman close to her age close the trunk of the car and head to the entrance, suitcase in hand.

"Emma!"

A woman in her early twenties turned at the sound of Kelly's shout, her auburn hair swinging with the movement. Her smile matched Kelly's, and she dropped her case to rush over to her friend. Emma had spent the summer at Azalea Plantation while she worked on her internship at the local promotion company. Kelly had been sad to see her leave, but knew Emma had several more internships to complete before she returned to her home in Citrus Beach to start her business. They had kept in touch and Kelly was delighted Emma had returned.

"Hey! I got your invitation and came early to offer my help." Emma answered the unasked question and grinned at Kelly, "You settling in okay?"

"Absolutely. The plantation feels like home, like I belong, and Lizzie's great." Kelly hugged Emma as she answered, thrilled to find her friend in front of her.

"Looks like Nora's been putting some meat on your bones. About time. Any ghostly visits since I left?"

Kelly nodded, remembering how Emma had been with her when she had come to Lizzie's, and soon after Lizzie had taken on the guardianship of the orphan. Together, they had helped solve a murder and had their first encounter with Elizabeth.

"You're not staying here. Can't you stay with me and Lizzie?" Kelly said, pointing to the suitcase Emma had dropped.

"Oh, I am. This is stuff for Nora from my mom. She thought Nora might want to have the old recipes and cookbooks she picked up when she was in Europe with my stepdad."

"Let me help," Kelly offered.

Walking back to the suitcase, they each grabbed a side handle and carried it into the house. Nora met them with a warm hug for Emma and a delighted clap of her hands when Emma told her what was in the case. With a show of strength, she easily picked up the case and headed to the kitchen, eager to investigate what Emma had brought her.

"Ok, now that's done, show me what's going on with the party plans."

"It's coming together perfectly. But I have something else to tell you." Kelly looked around and saw no one in the area, but she lowered her voice to little more than a stage whisper. "I've seen her."

"Elizabeth?"

Kelly nodded, and Emma grinned, eager to hear more.

It took little time for Emma and Kelly to catch up on what had been going on since Emma had left the plantation several months earlier. Kelly got Emma to tell her about her traveling adventures before she broke the news about Elizabeth and the locket brooch.

"You mean you actually had contact with Elizabeth? How exciting! She never appeared to me when I was here, but I know that you've seen her once before." Emma said.

"I've seen her several times since, but this is the first time she's appeared to only me and interacted with me. Usually, Lizzie's around, which makes sense because Lizzie is a direct descendant."

"Can you show me the brooch?"

Kelly didn't have to dig for the brooch, she had developed the habit of carrying it with her pinned to the waistband of her shorts. The clasp was strong, and she knew she wouldn't lose it. Somehow, she felt more connected to Elizabeth by wearing it. Unpinning it, she handed it to Emma.

"This is gorgeous. It's not some trinket, this is a family heirloom, and I bet it meant a lot to Elizabeth. You've got to find the locket that goes with it, and I'm going to help." As she spoke, Emma turned it over and noticed the engraved initials on the back of the brooch, which proved it belonged to Elizabeth.

"Fantastic. I was hoping you'd help. This is a big place for just me to look around and somehow, I think I need to find it for the party. I don't know why, but Elizabeth has seen the dress I am going to wear from the stash of gowns in the attic, and she seemed to approve of it. I've seen pictures of her in the dress and she was wearing the brooch. They seem to go together, and I think the dress was a favorite of Elizabeth.

Before Emma could answer Kelly, Nora came into the room with a list in her hand of chores she thought the two could help with.

"Sorry to put you to work Emma, but we're short on time," the older woman said as Kelly took the list from her.

"Not a problem. That's why I came; to help. Now, where do we start?" Emma answered as she peered at the list in Kelly's hands.

The next few hours flew by as the girls worked alongside Nora and Lizzie, getting things ready for the party. Halloween was now only a few days away, and they were running short of time. It wasn't until after dinner that they got a break, and they wandered outside to sit on one of the benches along the garden paths.

"So where have you looked for the brooch?" Emma asked as soon as she sat down.

"I've gone over every box in the attic, so I know the attic is not where it was lost or stored. Also, I looked in the older sections of the bed-and-breakfast. I figured the chance of it being in the newly remodeled areas would be slim, so the only places left are the sheds, gardens, and the old workers' quarters that are now cottages. You remember you stayed in one when you were here?"

Before Emma could answer Kelly, they heard the slamming of the car door and looked toward the parking lot to see Freddie standing by his car, staring in their direction.

"Is he still giving Lizzie problems?"

"Not so much. Freddie turned his attention to me. He's offended that Lizzie has taken me in with her guardianship and has me staying with her. He seems to think I'm intruding on his family title." Kelly shook her head as she answered.

"Well, don't let him get to you. I'm dying for a chance to put him in his place, so let him try something when I'm around." Emma put her hands on her hips and tilted her head back in a haughty manner, making Kelly giggle.

"I'd keep my eyes open around Freddie. I just don't trust him, and I wouldn't put it past him trying to do something underhanded to put me in bad graces with Lizzie and Nora."

The two women fell silent as they watched Freddie walk to the front door, knock, and let himself in. Kelly knew he wouldn't dare go farther than the reception area after the sound reprimand he'd gotten from Lizzie the last time he had been there.

Deciding that since Freddie was in the house, they were going to go in the opposite direction. Emma got it in her head that the answer was in the spookiest part of Azalea Plantation, and that was where they should start. The two girls got up and walked toward the older part of the garden where a family cemetery occupied a large corner of the property.

Emma and Kelly walked around the graveyard, starting in the far corner where the oldest gravesites were. Ancient headstones stood as silent sentinels; their inscriptions were worn by time but still legible. The girls took their time, brushing away leaves and dirt to reveal the names and dates, tracing the history of the Higgins family through the generations. The sun was low in the sky, casting long shadows that made the cemetery feel both serene and eerie.

"Look at this one," Emma said, pointing to an elaborate tombstone. "Elizabeth Higgins, beloved mother."

Kelly nodded, running her fingers over the carved letters. "She was amazing, wasn't she? To turn the plantation around like she did, and without using slaves like so many other plantation owners did. She was ahead of her time."

They moved from one gravestone to another, each told a story of the past. They were so engrossed in their task that they didn't notice Freddie had followed them and was watching from behind one of the taller monuments. But somebody else had noticed Freddie, and Elizabeth appeared near the girls just as he walked toward Emma and Kelly.

Emma gasped, her eyes widening in shock. She had caught glimpses of Elizabeth before and seen evidence of her visits, but this was the first time she had seen the spirit of Elizabeth Higgins in full form.

Kelly, more accustomed to Elizabeth's sudden appearances, smiled warmly at the ghost, wondering if Elizabeth would lead them to where the locket might be. Elizabeth, however, put her fingers to her lips, signaling for silence, and moved away from the two girls. As they followed her movements, they saw her circle behind Freddie. Both Emma and Kelly stifled the urge to laugh.

Elizabeth had lifted herself off the ground and was now hovering in the tree branches above Freddie. With a slight motion of her hand, she caused several large pinecones to fall, landing close to Freddie's feet. The man looked around, startled, but when the next two pinecones landed directly on his head, he squealed like a little girl and turned, running from the cemetery. Kelly and Emma burst out laughing, and Kelly waved to Elizabeth before she disappeared.

"That was incredible," Emma said, still giggling. "I've never seen anything like that."

"I know," Kelly replied and smiled. "Elizabeth has a way of keeping things interesting. But I don't think we're going to find anything here, other than entertainment."

"You're right," Emma agreed. "Besides, I have to admit it, I'm tired from the drive. Let's head over to Lizzie's house and get settled for the evening."

Kelly agreed, and the two girls followed Freddie's path from the cemetery to one of the garden paths that would lead to Lizzie's house. As they walked, they both grew silent, thinking of where else to look for the brooch.

Then, with a snap of her fingers, Kelly looked at Emma. "How can I be so stupid? Lizzie's house is the oldest building on the acreage. And it's the original homestead. It's where Elizabeth lived.

If we're going to find that locket, it's got to be somewhere in Lizzie's house."

"That makes perfect sense," Emma said, her eyes lighting up with renewed energy. "I'm not so tired now. We can spend the evening searching through the attic."

Emma linked her arm with Kelly's, and they picked up the pace, eager to start their search. The house loomed ahead of them, its windows glowing invitingly in the fading light. They entered through the back door, grabbed two flashlights from under the sink, ready to continue the search inside.

They headed up to the attic, the narrow stairs creaking under their weight. The attic was a treasure trove of old furniture, trunks, and boxes, each one a potential hiding place for the locket. Many were brought over from the bed-and-breakfast for storage and had never been looked through.

"We'll start with this side," Kelly said, pointing to a cluster of old trunks near the far wall. "And work our way over."

They opened the first trunk, revealing a collection of old clothes and hats. Emma pulled out a dress, holding it up to the light. "This must have belonged to Elizabeth. Look at the details."

Kelly nodded, but her focus was on the bottom of the trunk. She sifted through the layers of fabric, hoping to find the locket hidden beneath. But there was nothing but more clothes.

They moved on to the next trunk, then the next, finding only more clothes, old toys, and books. With each empty trunk, their frustration grew.

"Maybe we're looking in the wrong place," Emma said, sitting back on her heels and wiping sweat from her forehead. "What if it's not up here at all?"

"We can't give up now," Kelly said, her determination unwavering. "We still have half the attic to go."

They continued their search, working methodically through the attic. Each box and trunk they opened revealed more of the plantation's history, but not the locket they sought.

As they neared the end of their search, Kelly opened one last trunk. Inside, she found a small jewelry box. Her heart raced as she opened it, only to find a lock of dark wavy hair tied with a ribbon.

She sighed, sitting back and looking around the attic. "Maybe it's not up here."

Emma, who had been going through a stack of old books, looked over at Kelly. "It's getting late. Why don't we call it a night and try again after the Halloween party?"

Kelly nodded reluctantly. "Yeah, you're right. Let's head back down."

They gathered their things and made their way back down the stairs. As they reached the bottom, Kelly couldn't shake the feeling that they were close, that they had missed something important.

"We'll find it," Emma said, giving Kelly a reassuring smile. I know we will."

Kelly nodded, hoping her friend was right. As they headed back to their rooms to wash the dust away, Kelly couldn't help but glance back up the stairs, wondering if Elizabeth was watching and if she knew where the locket was hidden.

The time remaining until the Halloween party time sped by fast. There were plenty of projects that still needed to be completed, and everyone who worked for Lizzie was kept busy.

But in between chores and projects, Emma and Kelly continue to search for the missing locket. Harry thought it was great fun, and he joined them as often as he could get away with. But Harry had a habit of stealing and hiding items. More than once she had found an earring in her slipper or a stash of paperclips under the throw rug in Lizzie's office. Kelly was unsure of just how much help he was.

"Harry, put that down!" Kelly admonished the cat as she caught him stealing a bookmark from Lizzie's desk. The fat cat looked at her with disdain, but dropped the bookmark, only to pick up the earring that Lizzie had left lying on the desk. But this time he was too fast for Kelly, and he jumped from the desk and ran from the room.

"Lizzie's not going to be happy about that." Emma laughed as she watched the cat scurry away.

"I think Lizzie knows most of his hiding places. Besides, the things that he steals always show up eventually."

The two girls laughed and continued their search, only to be interrupted a few moments later by Nora asking them to do another errand.

"At this pace, we're never going to find the locket," Kelly moaned.

"Don't give up, Kelly, we'll find it."

And that's how their search went, nestled in between errands and party tasks.

But the one thing Kelly noticed when they had time for a more intensive search, Freddie always seemed to be around watching their movements. It was unnerving the way he seemed to show up at just the right moment, and his intense stare put Kelly's nerves on edge.

Freddie wasn't the only one that Kelly and Emma saw more frequently as they continued their search. The ghostly image of Elizabeth appeared to Kelly and Emma more than once, and Kelly found clusters of azalea blooms left several times.

She took them as signs of encouragement and always felt her mood boost after finding them. Emma thought the blossoms were clues from Elizabeth they should search in the area where they were left. But no matter how hard the girls searched, there was no sign of the locket.

The sun shone through the bedroom windows on the morning of the Halloween party, waking Kelly. She found herself with conflicting emotions. She was eager about the party, yet she was also disappointed that they had yet to find the locket. Kelly felt it was important that when she put the brooch on tonight with the dress, the locket should be attached. She did not know why she felt so driven to find the locket in time for the party, but by not finding it, she felt like she had let the ghost of Elizabeth Higgins down.

"Kelly, you wake?" Emma's voice cut into Kelly's thoughts, and she had a smile on her face as her friend opened her bedroom door.

Emma was already dressed, and knowing her friend so well, Kelly was sure she'd gone for a morning walk.

"You're up early. I suppose Nora's champing at the bit for us to get started," Kelly said to Emma as her friend sat on the end of her bed, nodding.

"She sent me up to get you. She's downstairs in the kitchen with another one of her infamous lists of chores. Who knew there was so much work in putting together a Halloween party?"

Kelly joined Emma's laughter and hopped out of bed. Moments later, she got dressed, pulling her hair up into a messy bun, with pink hair escaping into tendrils. When she came out of the bathroom, she found Harry sitting on the bed with Emma.

"Okay, let's get this day started," Kelly said.

When they entered the kitchen, Nora had a list ready for them, which she handed to Kelly. Looking over the list, Kelly was relieved to find it was more of a checklist than a to-do list. She noticed at the bottom of the list Nora had written to double-check the attic for props that might be used for additional decorating. She caught Emma's glance and pointed to Nora's note. It was perfect. Kelly and Emma wanted to check out the attic one last time, hoping to find the locket. It was the only place they hadn't double-checked.

Kelly grabbed a bottle of orange juice and filled a to-go cup. She was too excited to eat anything more and, motioning to Emma, she led the way out of the back door of Lizzie's house and headed to the bed-and-breakfast.

They wasted no time and headed directly for the attic. Kelly was the first one to reach the top of the stairs, and the first thing she saw was the azalea blossoms. There was a trail of them from the top of the stairs over to one trunk. As Kelly lifted the lid of the trunk, she realized it was the same one where she had found the dress she was going to wear tonight.

"You don't think the locket is still in the trunk, do you?" Emma asked.

"I don't see how. I've searched this trunk completely. Unless there's a hidden compartment somewhere, there's no way I missed it."

Kelly searched the trunk once again and, although she didn't find the locket, she found a beautiful shawl that would be perfect for the dress she was going to wear. While she searched the trunk, Emma was opening the hat boxes that were now stacked in the corner, the same boxes that Elizabeth had knocked over on Freddie. Closing the trunk, Kelly turned her attention to Emma and chuckled at the sight of her friend trying on the old hats.

But her laughter stopped when they opened the last box. Inside was a hat that was a perfect match to the dress she was going to wear. Maybe that's what Elizabeth wanted her to find, the accessories to the dress. She would still wear the brooch without the locket. The shawl and hat would complete her look, making it almost identical to the picture they had found of Elizabeth wearing the dress.

"I don't think we're going to find anything else. I'll take the shawl and hat and then we better check in with Nora and Lizzie." Kelly said.

The two friends were still giggling over the hats Emma had tried on as they made their way down the stairs. But their smiles disappeared when they reached the landing and found Freddie standing there staring at them, his arms crossed across his chest, his displeasure apparent.

Kelly and Emma stared at Freddie for a moment, trying to work their way around him. But he took a step back, lowering his arms from his chest to his hips, effectively blocking their way.

"I knew having you in this house would lead to no good. What are you trying to steal from the attic?" Freddie's voice dripped with suspicion.

Kelly shook her head, her mouth hanging open in disbelief. "Why would I steal? I have permission to be here, and I'm bringing these items down for the party."

"You seem to stick your nose in a lot of places around here. Places that should be for family members only. Not you."

Kelly gasped at his words, astonished and hurt. Lizzie and Nora had never once made her feel like an outsider, not since the first day she arrived. But with one breath, Freddie had isolated her and made her feel unwelcome.

"You're a real creep, Freddie," Emma hissed at him, taking Kelly's hand and giving it a supportive squeeze. "If you have a problem, maybe you should talk to Lizzie."

Freddie sneered, stepping closer. "You don't belong here, Kelly. This is my family's home. You're just an outsider Lizzie took pity on."

Kelly finally found her voice, standing tall. "Lizzie and Nora have made it clear that I'm welcome here. If you have an issue, take it up with them. Not me."

Emma's anger flared. "And what are you doing sneaking up on us? Trying to cause trouble, Freddie?"

"That's what I'd like to know, too," Lizzie's voice came from behind Freddie, and her cousin jumped, not expecting to see her.

"Girls, head downstairs. There's still plenty for you to do. Kelly, is there anything else I can bring down for you?" Lizzie addressed the girls and simultaneously clarified that Kelly was welcome to anything she wanted from the attic.

Kelly and Emma skirted around Freddie. There was a showdown coming between the two cousins, and they didn't want to be caught in the middle. As they hurried down the hall, Kelly looked back and saw Lizzie jam her hands on her hips and stare down at her cousin. As she watched, the shimmering figure of Elizabeth appeared by Lizzie's side, mimicking Lizzie's pose.

Kelly smiled at the ghost and gave a discreet wave. Then she noticed Freddie had lost all the color in his face and was shaking. Judging from his reaction, Kelly sensed this was the first time he'd seen Elizabeth up close and personal. Emma pulled Kelly's hand, and she turned to hurry after her friend, leaving the three Higgins behind to sort out their differences.

The girls joined Nora in the kitchen, and Emma quickly filled the older woman in on what was happening upstairs. Nora said nothing, just pursed her lips tightly and frowned. Kelly had seen Nora step in as a moderator between the cousins several times to keep the peace. But Kelly had a feeling even Nora's peacemaking wouldn't help this time.

It seemed like an eternity, but finally, they heard the front door slam, and a few moments later, Lizzie walked into the kitchen.

"Freddie sends his regrets, but he will not be attending the party tonight," she stated, giving Kelly a wink. Her tone invited no questions, and Kelly wisely said nothing. Nora gave a nod of understanding before taking charge, brushing the incident away as if it were insignificant. There were more important things to be done for the party that was only hours away.

"Let's focus on making tonight a success," Nora said, her voice firm. "Kelly, Emma, we need to finalize the decorations in the main hall. Let's get to it."

As they set off to work, Kelly couldn't help but feel a lingering tension. Freddie's words had stung, but the support from Lizzie and Nora fortified her resolve. She was part of this family, and she was determined to prove it.

Kelly held the picture she had found in the family photo album of Elizabeth, dressed in the gown she held in her arms. Kelly didn't want to just wear the gown. She wanted to create the essence of the time; from her hairstyle, though she couldn't do a thing about the pink hair color, to the accessories. There was the hat from the attic, and Lizzie had given her a feathered fan. She had found a pair of shoes in a theater prop outlet and, of course, she had Elizabeth's brooch.

She finally had her hair how she wanted when Lizzie knocked on her door.

"Do you need a hand with the buttons on your dress, Kelly?" Lizzie asked as she opened the door. "It's almost time to go over to the main house. Nora and Emma are waiting for us."

"Thanks, Lizzie. I don't know how I would handle all these tiny buttons. I guess that's why they had lady's maids, huh?"

Lizzie laughed and then helped Kelly lift the folds of the dress up and over her head. The gown was a perfect fit, and Lizzie made quick work of the long row of pearl buttons that ran from the neckline to past her waist. Smoothing the folds of the dress, Kelly turned so Lizzie could see her.

"Well?"

"Kelly, you look fantastic. You could have easily been a southern belle, the lady of the house. It's like you were meant to wear the dress. Here, let me help you with the hat. Do you know how to use a hatpin?" Lizzie asked as she picked up the ornate hat and pulled the hat pin out for Kelly to see.

"Not a clue. That looks dangerous!"

Lizzie laughed, and then expertly adjusted the hat to show Kelly off to her best advantage. Kelly held her breath as the hat pin was used and then turned back to the mirror to see the results of Lizzie's handy work. Lizzie's smile of approval reflected at them from the mirror, and Kelly couldn't help but admire the gown the other woman wore.

"You look pretty stunning yourself."

"It's fun to dress up, but I don't think I'd like to wear these dresses every day."

"Oh, I don't know..." Kelly mused and grinned back at their reflection.

"Come on, let's get a move on before Nora comes looking for us."

Turning toward the door, Lizzie led the way out of the room. Kelly took one more look in the mirror and adjusted the folds of her gown. As she did, she was thrilled to find a hidden pocket sewn into the side seam. This was probably used for a delicate handkerchief, but Kelly had a more modern use in mind. Grabbing her cell phone from the dresser, she stuffed it into her pocket. It barely fit, and as she adjusted the pocket to make room, she felt something hard along the inner seam.

"Kelly!"

Pulling her hand from the pocket, Kelly hurried after Lizzie, eager to see the costumes Emma and Nora would be wearing.

Kelly had to stop and stare at the sight before her eyes. Dusk had set, and the pathway to the entry of the bed-and-breakfast was lined with lit jack-o'-lanterns. Strings of lights hung from the Oak trees, giving the tendrils of Spanish moss a spooky glow. The front doors were wide open, and she could hear the mixture of the guests' voices and the music from the small band that was set up in the gardens. Electric candles flickered in the windows and the caterers mingled among the guests, dressed in period costume.

Thrilled at the sight in front of her, Kelly laughed and moved forward, eager to see Emma in costume. She saw Nora first, dressed as a housekeeper from the turn of the past century. It was perfect for her, and she played the part well, keeping the staff in motion and seeing to the guests' needs.

"Kelly! You look fantastic." Emma greeted Kelly with a hug and then stood back to take in the sight of her friend. "Kelly, you were born at the wrong time, that dress is perfect for you. It looks like it was made especially for you."

"You look great, too. Are those riding clothes?"

"Yeah, I'm not one for fancy gowns. I could never pull it off like you and Lizzie. She looks wonderful, too. Like the lady of the manor."

"You both look great. Now, go and mingle, enjoy yourselves. You've worked hard to make this party a success." Nora said as she walked up to them. The girls didn't need to be told twice, and they left Lizzie and Nora to join the rest of the guests.

For the next several hours, they had the time of their lives. As the night wore on, the music got livelier and the voices louder. The staff used the scripts they had been given to share ghost stories and keep the atmosphere on the spooky Halloween side. The legend of Elizabeth Higgins and how she had stolen a fortune from a gang of train robbers, fooled her abusive husband, and fled in the dark of the night with her children to return to her family home was the favorite story to hear. Elizabeth then took over the running of the family farm and turned it into a success. But she supposedly never used the stolen money, and the tale goes it is hidden somewhere on Azalea Plantation.

As the night went on, several rowdier guests suggested they should search for the treasure, but Lizzie discouraged them and directed their attention to more food or drink. The party became overwhelming for Kelly as the night wore on. She didn't know as many of the guests as Emma did from doing an internship in town and often felt like a third wheel when Emma was catching up with a guest.

It was on one such occasion when Kelly needed a few moments of quiet time. She slipped into the library and sank into her favorite chair in front of the fireplace. She closed her eyes for a moment and instantly felt the weight of the fat cat jumping onto her lap.

"Harry, what are you doing here?"

Kelly opened her eyes and stared at the cat, who was supposed to be shut up in Lizzie's house. Harry gave a mournful meow and turned his head to the books on the table. Sitting on top of the books was a stem of azalea blossoms.

Kelly got to her feet, and with the folds of the gown swirling, walked over to pick up the flower blooms. Usually, when she saw the flowers, she felt a tinge of excitement at the prospect of an encounter with Elizabeth's ghost. But as she brushed the soft petals against her cheek, she felt guilty. She had failed to find the locket, and it seemed to her as if she had let Elizabeth down.

Harry's meow and the feel of him rubbing against her leg through the gown brought Kelly's attention to his antics. Harry was moving between Kelly and the sliding glass door that led out into one of the many private gardens at Azalea Plantation. He meowed again, and there was no ignoring the cat's tone. He wanted Kelly to follow him.

"What's up, Harry?"

Kelly asked as she walked to the door and slid it open. Harry's answer was to take a few steps into the garden and then turn back and meow at Kelly. She was familiar with the cat's method of communication, or with "Harry demands", and she followed him as he led her to a stone bench positioned by a small fountain. Harry jumped on the bench and waited.

"Ok, I'm here. What do you want, you silly cat?"

Harry reached a paw out and pulled at the gown. Sitting on the bench, he was in the perfect position to reach the folds of the dress that hid the pocket. His head followed his paw, and before Kelly knew what he was doing, the cat used his teeth to pull on her phone that hid in her pocket.

"Now seems like a funny time to want your picture taken. You're such a ham!"

Kelly chuckled as she pushed the cat's head out of the pocket and picked up her phone. Harry loved to have his picture taken and would often steal Kelly's or Lizzie's phone from them to get his point across. He would grab the corner of the phone with his teeth, get a grip around the protective case on the phone, and drag it away. More than once, he had stepped on the screen and managed to take a selfie. But this time, he ignored Kelly as she focused her camera on him and pawed at her pocket again. Puzzled, Kelly pushed him away from her pocket and shoved her hand inside to see what Harry was so interested in. Her pocket was empty without the phone, but as she removed her hand, Kelly felt the hard object tangled in the seam.

Curious, Kelly picked at the seam, trying to release the object from the stitches. Finally, in frustration, she pulled the pocket out of the skirt. After a few more tries, she saw a glimmer of metal within the silk of the pocket lining. At the same moment she saw the metal, she sensed she was being watched, and looked up to find the shimmer of Elizabeth's form. As she became more discernible, Elizabeth nodded at Kelly and smiled encouragingly. With a final tug of the material, Kelly freed the metal object and watched it drop onto the bench.

"The locket! I found the locket, Elizabeth." Kelly's voice echoed her glee. She hadn't let Elizabeth down.

The smile on Elizabeth's face said more than words could. After a moment, the ghost pointed to the locket and then looked at Kelly.

"Do you want me to open the locket?"

Kelly was already trying to open it along the seam of the metal. It took several attempts, but finally, she found the locket's latch and pushed. Slowly, the locket opened to reveal two pictures, one on each side of the locket. Kelly squinted to see the faded photos. She grinned when she recognized the first one and glanced up at Elizabeth.

"This is a lovely photo of you. You look very happy." She whispered to the shimmery figure.

Then Kelly looked at the other side of the locket and gasped.

While Kelly stared, fascinated, at the locket in her open hand, Harry had jumped down from his perch at her side and disappeared. Kelly didn't even notice. But when he reappeared, he wasn't alone.

"Kelly?"

Kelly jumped at the pressure of a hand on her shoulder and looked up to find Lizzie and Nora standing by her side. Harry had brought support. Kelly looked down at the locket that had fallen from her hand and landed on her lap, still not grasping what she saw. Silently, she picked it up and handed it to Lizzie.

"How is this possible? Nora, do you see what I see?" Lizzie asked, looking back and forth from the locket to Kelly. She handed the locket to Nora for her opinion.

"How did you do this, Kelly?" Nora asked after studying the tiny pictures in the locket.

"I didn't do anything. I just found it in the folds of my gown pocket. The locket was Elizabeth's. I found pictures of her wearing her brooch and the locket was attached. I've been looking for the locket since I found the brooch. Emma has been helping me."

Kelly looked back at the locket in Nora's hand and swallowed hard. "But what does it mean?"

Nora and Lizzie stared back at Kelly, but they weren't who she was talking to. Her words were for Elizabeth, who seemed to glow even brighter at Kelly's question. The ghost pointed to the locket and then at Kelly with no words spoken. She seemed to want Kelly to look at the locket again. When Kelly did, she saw a faded image of a young girl dressed in a gown from the late 1800s. The faded image was like looking into a cloudy mirror. Kelly closed her eyes tightly for a few seconds, but when she opened them, she still saw herself in black and white, looking back at her from the locket.

"I don't understand. How did a picture of me get in Elizabeth's locket? Is this a mean joke on Freddie's part?"

"If Freddie is involved, then the joke is on him. I think it's pretty obvious what is going on," Lizzie spoke up and looked at Elizabeth's shimmering form for confirmation. The specter gave a nod and a slight smile. "Kelly, somehow you are related to Elizabeth Higgins."

Kelly stared at Lizzie, not understanding what she meant. "No, you're wrong. I may not know who my parents were, but I know I was born in Maine. How could I be related to Elizabeth when her family—you and Freddie—are from the south? Didn't you say her family stayed close to Azalea Plantation all these years?" Kelly shook her head vigorously, denying the possibility of the connection between herself and the Higgins family.

"Yes, our family records say that Elizabeth's children, and consequent generations, stayed in this area. But you can't deny the picture in the locket. Whoever that woman is, she is the spitting image of you. There is a link between you."

As Kelly, Lizzie, and Nora watched, Elizabeth made a motion with her hands, pointing to herself and then Kelly. Then she gently tossed a handful of azalea blossoms in the air. When the petals landed on the ground at Kelly's feet, they spelled the word Mine. With a gasp, Kelly looked back at Elizabeth, but the apparition was gone.

"We'll find the connection, Kelly. I promise." Lizzie reached out and gave Kelly a hug of reassurance. Nora nodded in agreement.

Kelly took a deep breath, still processing everything. "Maybe we can start by looking through the old family records again and see if there's any mention of Elizabeth having other children or relatives who might have moved north."

Nora nodded thoughtfully. "And we should check any old letters or diaries that might have been left behind. There could be clues hidden in them."

Lizzie smiled, squeezing Kelly's hand. "We'll figure this out. Elizabeth brought us all together for a reason, and we'll uncover the truth."

Kelly felt a surge of determination. "Yes, we'll find the answers. And who knows, maybe it will lead us to more about my past."

The three of them looked down at the soft pink azalea blossoms, a silent promise of the journey ahead.

Victoria L.K. Williams

Thanks for reading Harry's Haunted Halloween. I hope you enjoyed getting to know Harry, Kelly, and the others. The story ending twist was a surprise even to me, and I can't wait to explore where it will take me with the rest of the series.

If you'd like to read more of Lizzie and Harry's mysteries and discover how Kelly became part of their home, you can read the first two books in Professor Higgin's Investigates series, Thyme to Depart and Catnip Caper.

To learn more about my books, please visit www.VictoriaLKW illiams.com.

THE AUTHORS

Lily Stirling

Sharon E. Buck

Victoria Williams

Kristen Elizabeth

Bellamina Court

Juliet Sidonie

6 Great Authors

Sharon E. Buck

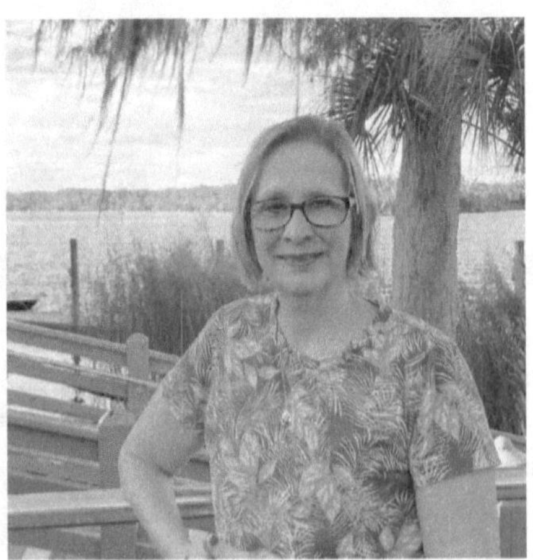

Ghouls Just Wanna Have Fun

Sharon is the brilliant mind behind three cozy mystery series set in that little slice of paradise known as the Northeast Florida Bermuda Triangle—where Jacksonville, St. Augustine, and Palatka (a.k.a Pothole and Palm Park) beckon tourists to tread carefully. She weaves together humor, heart, plenty of sass, and just the right amount of snark in every story. While her characters might be a tad over the top—some might even call them quirky—Sharon guarantees you'll recognize a few of them from real life. When she's not plotting fictional crimes, she's likely lost in a good book. With her knack for turning the mundane into the mysterious and a sharp wit that keeps readers chuckling, Sharon promises to keep you guessing—and laughing—until the very last page.

For a free book, you know you want one (www.SharonEBuck.com) be sure to sign up for Sharon's twice-a-month newsletter where there's plenty of fun and laughter including her very popular "Fun Fact About Me You May Not Know" section. She promises not to give your email address to the car warranty people!

Sleuthing off for now with a wink and a clue. May the snark be with you.

Getting in touch:

Email: sharon@sharonebuck.com

Website: SharonEBuck.com

Bellamina Court

Murder at the Manor

Bellamina is a mystery writer, focusing on cozy and soft-boiled mysteries. With a passion for crafting engaging stories featuring strong, independent women.

A self-proclaimed zookeeper, Bellamina spent the last two decades as a stay-at-home mom to seven children. She currently shares her home with four dogs, three cats, two daughters, and one husband. When she's not penning her next whodunit, she enjoys sitting on the beach under a palm tree, sipping a margarita.

To learn more about her captivating mysteries, visit www.Bella minaCourt.com and subscribe to her newsletter for updates, sneak peeks, and exclusive content.

Getting in touch:

Email: bellamina@bellaminacourt.com

Website: BellaminaCourt.com

Kristen Elizabeth

Love, Lies, and Lavender

I hope you enjoyed this collection of short stories. This was a passion project brought together from an unlikely group of strangers turned friends. If you enjoyed the stories and want to shout them to all the rooftops, please rate and review them on the sites you frequent. We'd love to hear from you!

Love, Lies, and Lavender is the first published work from Kristen Elizabeth. While working on the project, she fell in love with the cast and is now planning a series centering on Ellie and her floral shop mysteries. When Kristen is not writing and genre-hopping, she can be found spending time with her children, reading, and watching anime. To follow Kristen Elizabeth and her shenanigans, visit www.AuthorKristenElizabeth.com for exclusive content and social media links.

Getting in touch:

Email: author@authorkristenelizabeth.com

Website: AuthorKristenElizabeth.com

Julie E. Sidonie

Mystery of the Missing Heirloom

Through conversation and stories, two friends who like old movies, mysteries, and history started talking about writing a book that featured these elements. One friend has two books published about her mother, Doris Markham. Doris, who lived in Kansas City in the 1930s, experienced some of the stories told in this book. The other friend thought that a detective inspired by Doris Markham would be a great place to begin this writing adventure. As time progressed, the friends developed the Miss Markham Mystery Series. The main character, much like her real-life inspiration, is spunky, hard-headed, and fearless. The name Juliet E. Sidonie is a combination of the two authors' grandmother's and great-grandmother's names. For more about this series, visit their website, MissMarkhamMysteries.com.

Getting in touch:

Email: jsidonie@protonmail.com

Website: MissMarkhamMysteries.com

Lily Stirling

Holt Jacobs and the Halloween Splash

Congratulations!

Not only have you read six mysteries, but you've also earned your Super Sleuth badge...next up, you can become a Private Investigator.

When the opportunity for this cozy collection happened, my mind was focused on Holt Jacobs's Christmas mystery, *A Not So Cozy Christmas*. I didn't want to throw off Holt's current timeline, so after an appropriate amount of staring at the wall and muttering to myself, I decided a college prequel was the best option. Throughout the books, Holt being a college lifeguard has been referenced so this was the perfect opportunity to explore that.

Holt Jacobs and the Halloween Splash was a fantastic introduction to Holt for readers who'd never experienced him before, while also being tons of fun for readers who have grown to love Holt as much as I do.

For more information about the Holt Jacobs Mystery Series check out my website at *LilyStirling.com*. Also, I'd love to hang out with you! On my website, you can sign up for my newsletter and receive delightful every-other-week emails, plus a free copy of *Holt Jacobs and the Mystery of the Missing Sunglasses*, which leads right into Holt's first novel, *A Not So Shocking Murder*.

Hope to see you there!

Lily Stirling

Getting in touch:

Website: *LilyStirling.com*

Victoria L.K. Williams

Harry's Haunted Halloween

I hope you have enjoyed our Halloween Collection. This is more than a book to us. It is an opportunity to give back to the writing community by supporting young writers! The six of us started with an idea and it grew not only into a book for you to enjoy, but friendships that will be lasting.

My husband and I recently retired, giving me more time to devote to my writing passion. When I'm not busy crafting my next captivating mystery, you can find me strolling the peaceful paths around the lake near our home, curled up with a good book, tending to my colorful garden, or working on my latest needlepoint project. And of course, I'm never without the company of our two beloved, albeit demanding, feline companions.

In my cozy world, no mystery goes unsolved! Whether you're in the mood for a modern-day caper or a paranormal puzzle, my quirky, clever sleuths will stop at nothing to crack the case - all while tending to their beautiful gardens, running their charming businesses, cuddling their adorable fur babies, and balancing family and friendships with their sleuthing adventures.

So, grab a cup of your favorite beverage, get comfy, and prepare to be swept away by my cozy mysteries with a tropical twist. Can you solve the mystery before my sleuth? Discover my full collection of sunny sleuths and beachy bedlam at VictoriaLKWilliams .com. Happy reading, my friends!

Getting in touch:

Website: VictoriaLKWilliams.com